OVE
E

CU00727458

OVER THE EDGE

AUDREY HOPKINS

Scripture Union
130 City Road, London EC1V 2NJ

By the same author:
Joanna's Journey – a Leopard Book
Love and Laura – Impressions

© Audrey Hopkins 1993
First published 1993

ISBN 0 86201 789 0

British Library Cataloguing-in-Publication Data.
A catalogue record for this book is available from the British
Library.

Phototypeset by Intype, London.
Printed and bound in Great Britain by Cox and Wyman Ltd,
Reading.

~ 1 ~

'The trouble with you, Lisa Fisher, is the size of your mouth!' Carrie Rogers snapped, tossing her blonde pony-tail and turning her back on the slim, brown-haired girl who barred her way.

'The trouble with Codfish is her nosey-parker nose and elephant's ears!' Joy Thomas giggled, linking arms with Carrie and starting to move her away. 'We don't have to go that way, or listen to her!'

'Don't turn your back on me!' Lisa warned, her fists clenching and unclenching in time to her heartbeat. 'I said, don't turn your back!'

'And if I do?' Carrie asked, grinning over her shoulder to show Joy and Tracy that Lisa's threats didn't worry her at all – even though they did! No-one wanted a stand-up fight with Lisa Fisher. She usually won!

'What is the great and mighty Lisa Fisher going to do about it?' she went on, almost sure that Lisa wouldn't do anything with a crowd watching.

She couldn't have been more wrong. Carrie's grin turned to an open mouth and a howl of pain as both Lisa's fists thudded into her back, just between her shoulder blades, sending her and Tracy reeling against the changing-room lockers.

'You bitch!' Joy gasped, hurrying to comfort Carrie and Tracy. 'You want locking up! Didn't anybody teach you how to behave in your bit of the gutter?'

'Like who?' Carrie sneered. 'She doesn't have anybody. What do you expect from somebody who's been dragged up?'

Lisa couldn't believe it! All she'd done was ask for change for 50p and she'd landed in the middle of World War Three! Everyone was ganging up on her like some sort of criminal! Perhaps she should have got down on her knees and begged for it!

'Get lost,' she growled.

'Don't worry, we will!' Carrie said, then everyone turned their back and started to move away – taking sides as usual. And, as usual, no-one sided with Lisa!

Lisa turned on her heels and ran up the stairs two at a time, only stopping at the end of the upstairs corridor to watch them cross to the dining hall. The Main Block was built on three sides of a large paved area with an island of small trees and shrubs in the centre. The girls were allowed to stroll in the area at break as long as they kept away from the drive that swept from the front gate through green lawns and ornamental flower beds.

The drive made a right turn at the dining room on the end of the right wing and opened out into a large out-of-bounds car park. The girls called the area 'the Prison Yard' and morning break the 'Exercise Period'.

The dining room was on the ground floor opposite Lisa and from her vantage point on the second floor she could see the queues waiting for hot buttered toast and drinks. The kitchen staff ran a canteen at break because many of the girls travelled quite a distance and left home early in the morning.

Lisa was hungry. Her stomach gave a loud gurgle that echoed down the empty corridor. She had her lunch money in her bag but she couldn't go down to the canteen, or to the vending machine on the bottom corridor. That was why she wanted the change – because the machine had run out. It took a visit to the school office to claim lost change and the further she kept away from there, the better!

Lisa Fisher was not the most popular girl in the school! She could see the group of sympathisers gathering round Carrie, all peering up at the windows hoping to spot 'Fishface' and make faces at her. Well, they wouldn't have that pleasure!

The empty school was patrolled at break but Lisa had plenty of hiding places, one of them right there on the corridor. Just outside the Maths room were several heavy book cupboards and one hid a narrow space between two extra pillars that supported the roof. There had been a doorway there, once, that led into a store-room but it had been boarded up, Lisa calculated that the entrance door was in the Maths room itself so that it was convenient for Miss Dodds.

She hated Miss Dodds! Everyone, at least once in their life, comes face to face with instant 'Yuk!', the type of person that sets teeth on edge before they even speak! It was like that with Lisa and Miss Dodds. War was declared every time they came face to face and sometimes they only had to be in the same room for sparks to fly.

Lisa held her breath and squeezed past the pillars into the space behind the cupboard. It wasn't very roomy but it was all hers. The floor was littered with chocolate wrappers and crisp bags and the plywood back was filled with comments in black felt tip. Lisa had written quite a lot over the last eighteen months. Nearly all the comments began 'I HATE' and some were rude and unrepeatable, 'I HATE MISS DODDS' figured more than most with 'I HATE SCHOOL' a close second.

Right in the middle, in red felt tip and in the same

writing were the words . . . 'I HATE LISA FISHER'.

'Sometimes I do,' she whispered aloud. 'I do hate myself!'

The click-clack of high heels on the tiled floor kept her motionless until the teacher passed. The door to the Maths room opened and closed and she could hear Miss Dodds moving about in the store-room.

Lisa relaxed, pressing her lower back against the boarded up door and her toes against the base of the cupboard. From her pocket she took a strip of chewing gum, popping it into her mouth and dropping the wrapper onto the floor. It wasn't a slice of toast but it was better than nothing.

She thought about Carrie Rogers. They had been best friends in the first year of Bourne High School and part of a great crowd for some of the second. Everybody liked Carrie, especially the teachers. She was that sort of girl – the sort that always wore a well-ironed blouse, a bow in her ponytail and shoes you could see your face in! Carrie always had a crowd around her, a crowd that didn't want Lisa Fisher!

'Who needs them?' she muttered, then jumped as the shrill buzzer brought noise and bustle back to the corridor.

Lisa waited until it was quiet again, then eased out of her hiding place and slipped into the Maths room, only moments after the last one in and just before Miss Dodds closed the door. She ignored the hostile glare from Carrie Rogers and slumped in her desk, ready for the day's battle with Miss Dodds.

The teacher cleared her throat several times and shuffled papers and books on her desk until she found her register. Miss Dodds always marked it at the beginning of her lessons to make sure they were all there, or that's what she said. Lisa knew it was really to make sure *she* was there, because sometimes she wasn't! Miss Dodds picked on her, that was it.

How Lisa hated Miss Dodds! She was so efficient and liked everyone to know it. When the register was done she turned her attention to the pile of books, handing them out and making sarcastic comments to one or two girls. Miss Dodds was nice to those who were good at her subject, like Carrie Rogers. Lisa could feel the sneer forming on her face. All the teachers liked Carrie.

Miss Dodds came to the end of the pile.

'Lisa Fisher! No homework from you . . . again!'

Lisa sighed, shifted her position and stared at Miss Dodds, chewing her gum defiantly.

Miss Dodds picked up the waste basket and held it out. There was a long silence before Lisa took out the sticky mess, held it aloft for a few seconds then dropped it in.

'Well, have you anything to say?' Miss Dodds asked when the bin was back in place.

Lisa propped her chin on her hands and yawned, noisily.

'Like what?' she asked, her eyebrows raised.

'Like . . . I haven't done my homework because . . .!' Miss Dodds prompted, turning a faint shade of pink.

'I haven't done my homework because . . . because I was sick? . . . because I had a nasty accident with a can of Coke? . . . because I couldn't do it . . . or because I couldn't be bothered?' Lisa answered, sitting up straight and staring Miss Dodds in the eye. 'Do any of these take your fancy?'

Miss Dodds turned a very unattractive shade of crimson. Several girls giggled and one or two squirmed with embarrassment but most of the class groaned.

'Another maths lesson without any maths!' somebody at the back of the room muttered.

'I wish she'd give up. She's a real pain!' someone else said and there was a general murmur of agreement from the rest of the class. Lisa held her breath. She'd done it again . . . forced a confrontation that could only have one outcome – more trouble for Lisa. Why couldn't she just sit still and say nothing?

Unfortunately for Miss Dodds, once Lisa Fisher had started a course of action it was impossible to stop. Her reputation for hardness and nerve would be lost and people might catch a glimpse of the other Lisa, the one that cried a lot.

'Just who do you think you are talking to, Lisa?' Miss Dodds asked quite calmly, hoping to prevent episode two of the drama.

There was a tense silence. No one breathed while Lisa cast her eyes around the room then turned her attention back to the teacher.

'No one in particular,' she said, shrugging her shoulders and raising her eyebrows in what she imagined was an 'I couldn't care less' expression.

The class gasped once, then resumed holding its breath.

'I will not put up with your rudeness, Lisa!' Miss Dodds said, rising to her full five feet behind her desk.

'Tough!' Lisa drawled.

That was the final straw for Miss Dodds. Determined not to enter into a shouting match with Lisa she ordered her out of the room.

'Remove your offensive self, Lisa Fisher,' she said. 'And wait outside Mrs Foster's room!'

Mrs Foster was Head of Year 10 and quite fierce. Most of the girls trembled at the thought of being sent to her but Lisa wasn't worried . . . for the simple reason that she wasn't going!

She stood up, slamming down her desk lid and knocking all her books onto the floor. She picked them up, very slowly, even lingering over her English book to read a few sentences.

'Lisa! Will you please leave so that I can start my lesson?' Miss Dodds asked, still trying to keep things as peaceful as possible. Lisa sauntered down the aisle, swinging her bag over her shoulder and banging against as many desks as she could, making sure she bumped Carrie Rogers as she passed.

'Creep,' she growled.

Carrie bit her lip, staring straight ahead, avoiding trouble and unwilling to be part of the disruption. To Carrie, her reputation among the teachers was all-important. She meant to be Head Girl one day and stupid Lisa Fisher wasn't going to spoil her chances.

Lisa flung back her head and marched to the door, only turning to glare at the class when it was open and she was half-way through it.

'Have a nice day!' she jeered, then left, slamming the door so hard that the windows rattled.

Lisa had no intention of waiting outside Mrs Foster's room. She had been there so many times that year that the teachers had run out of things to say to her. Her footsteps echoed down the long corridor. Everyone was in lessons except a small-fry out on an errand. The girl walked on the left as the rules dictated and almost scraped the wall to avoid contact with Lisa. She tried not to look at the bigger girl but couldn't help a sidelong glance as they passed.

'What are you looking at?' Lisa snapped, grabbing the girl's arm and stopping her.

'Nothing,' the girl whispered, her voice almost gone in fear of Lisa. 'I'm just going to the Art room for Mr Brown.'

'What have you got in your pocket?'

The girl looked from right to left along the empty corridor, hoping for help.

'Nothing,' she said.

'Yes you have!' Lisa snapped, shaking the girl by the

arm. 'Give it here!'

'It's my bus fare.'

'It isn't now!'

Lisa gave the girl a shove, once she had taken her 48p, then ran to the cloakroom for her ski jacket. She left by the front doors, marching through the ornamental entrance hall with its sunken garden and fossil-filled marbled floor then out across the Prison Yard and down the drive.

To her left the dinner ladies busied themselves in the dining room and across the drive, to her right, she could see Miss Dodds out in the upper corridor where she herself had stood at break, watching her go. Lisa stared straight at her then waved, turning the wave into a rude sign as she passed through the gates.

Once away from school and hidden in the back streets of the older part of town Lisa's whole body changed shape. Her shoulders slumped forward and she seemed to shrink at least two inches. She dragged her feet along the pavement, letting her head drop almost to her chest. She couldn't stop the tears that ran down her cheeks but they were hidden by the curtain of dull brown hair that straggled each side of her thin face.

Lisa felt so alone, even though there were people all around her. She knew it was possible to be lonely in a crowd because she always was. She was always on the edge, outside of things, never belonging.

'I don't belong anywhere . . . nobody cares!' she had shrieked that morning as she left her foster home. Mr and Mrs Carmichael, her latest set of foster parents, ('Call us Mom and Pop, Lisa,' yuk!) had tried to reason with her but she had left, slamming the door behind her. Lisa had slammed a lot of doors lately!

With a sudden change of mood she brushed away her tears with her coat sleeve and ran, dodging between shoppers and traffic until she arrived at the pier, gasping for breath. The tide was in, swirling around the encrusted stanchions that held up the ornate Victorian pier and the promenade was empty but for the resident pigeons pecking at nothing and the wheeling seagulls overhead.

Lisa liked the town in the season when the promenade and beaches were crowded with holiday-makers but she loved it now, out of season, when the wind blew spray against her face and the seagulls hung motionless in the air, riding the gusts. She loved the empty beach, the smell of drying seaweed and the feeling of freedom and space.

Sometimes, on really bad days, she would go down onto the beach and run and run until she was exhausted. Once . . . she had thought about running into the sea until it closed over her, but a dog had come along and taken her mind off things for a while. He had liked her just as she was and had followed her home but – as expected – Lisa Fisher couldn't have anything she wanted and the dog warden had collected the stray.

By lunch-time all her dinner money, plus the 48p she had acquired, had disappeared into the machines in the amusement arcade. It was open all year round for the local people and Lisa spent most of her time there when she walked out of school – which was quite often.

She won a few times but, as always, the thought of winning lots of money kept her feeding coins into the slots. She walked to the end of the pier and back, twice, and spent half an hour perched on a sink in the toilets before going back into the arcade to watch other people waste money. Some of the computer games were for two people and she was always ready to be a partner.

At five o'clock she set off home, on foot, her stomach protesting about its lack of food. Apart from the chewing gum she hadn't eaten since breakfast and half of that she'd left on the table when she stormed out.

'Where have you been?' Mr Carmichael asked when

she strolled in.

'School!'

'No, you haven't!'

'Why bother to ask if you already know?'

'Who do you think you're talking to . . . ?'

It was the usual conversation, the one she had most of the time with most of the people she met, and one that always ended the same way.

'This is boring,' she said. 'Why can't you leave me alone?'

'How can you expect to be left alone when you're totally irresponsible and incapable of behaving?'

Lisa sighed and rolled her eyes as Mrs Carmichael tried to put an end to the growing tension.

'Let's talk about it after tea, shall we?' she suggested, spooning potatoes and peas onto plates already served with pork chops and apple sauce, 'I don't spend the afternoon cooking for it to be spoiled. Sit down and eat while it's hot, then we'll sort things out.'

Lisa's mouth watered as she moved to her place. It seemed weeks since breakfast instead of just hours and she had to admit that her present foster mother was a very good cook.

'I'm really hungry,' she said, picking up her knife and fork and starting to cut through the tender chop.

'Just a minute . . .' Mr Carmichael butted in. 'I haven't finished. Mrs Foster rang so we know all about . . .'

Before he could finish Lisa's temper flared. The knife and fork clattered onto the table and her chair toppled as she leapt to her feet.

'So what!' she yelled. 'What's it to do with you? You're not my parents, so get lost!'

As she spat out the last two words she swept her plate across the table and fled before it crashed onto the floor and smashed, scattering peas and gravy in all directions. Mr Carmichael banged on the table and stood up as Lisa left the room and she could hear him as she took the stairs three at a time.

'She has to learn a bit of respect if she's to stay. I won't have . . .'

Lisa didn't wait to hear any more. It was nothing new.

Once in her bedroom, out of breath and feeling sick, Lisa waited for the lecture that was sure to come when everybody had calmed down. She glared at herself in the dressing-table mirror, hating what she saw.

'You're ugly, Lisa Fisher,' she growled. 'Ugly!'

Her mouth turned down at the corners and her eyebrows came together in a frown that had become part of her face. Her hair hung in dull brown strands and an ugly pimple was ready to erupt on the end of her chin.

'Why would anyone like you?'

Her reflection didn't answer.

~ 2 ~

Carrie Rogers was walking along Bourne Road with Joy when Mr Carmichael drove Lisa to school the next morning. Lisa had demanded that she be allowed to go on the bus as usual but her foster parents weren't taking any chances.

The car was a vintage Volkswagen, restored and in beautiful condition. It was also bright red with a white streak down both sides – a unique car that everybody recognised.

It was raining and Carrie had her head down, holding her anorak hood to protect her curly fringe, but Joy saw the car and nudged Carrie, whispering something in her ear and pointing.

Lisa hoped that the car would splash both of them as it passed but Mr Carmichael steered well away from the gutter puddles.

'You can drop me here,' she said, gathering her belongings as they neared the school gates.

Mr Carmichael said nothing but turned into the drive and made for the car park that opened up behind the dining hall.

'I'd like to walk from here,' Lisa said.

'What you would like is quite unimportant Lisa. I said I'd see you to school and I'm doing just that,' Mr Carmichael said, turning off the engine and pulling on the hand-brake. 'It seems you're not to be trusted out on your own. You've run off five times since you came to live with us!'

Lisa said nothing but gathered her things and hurried out of the car. She was horrified when he got out too and walked with her. He looked so old fashioned. Carrie's father wore trendy shirts and jeans, or a light suit with the sleeves rolled up like an American detective. Mr Carmichael wore a ginger coloured hairy jacket and a waistcoat! He had gingery hair too, where it wasn't edged with grey and he walked like a sergeant major on parade, all straight backed and stuck-up. He was really embarrassing!

'We have to use the side door,' she said.

'Not today. The front please. That's the way you left yesterday, isn't it?'

'Are you going to hold my hand too?' she muttered.

Everyone could see as they walked into the hall where the Wicked Witch of the West was waiting, a sickly smile on her face as she met Mr Carmichael with an outstretched hand.

'Thank you, Mr Carmichael. Lisa, go and put your coat in the cloakroom and come straight back here,' Mrs Foster ordered.

'Yes, Mrs Foster,' Lisa lisped, adding a curtsey to her play-acting. She knew it annoyed the Year Head.

'That's enough, young lady. Get a move on!'

Lisa walked down the corridor with her head high, ignoring the whispers and giggles she met as she passed. Once around the corner she quickened her pace, pushing past the hoards making for their classrooms in the science block.

'Move!' she yelled at two who dawdled in front of

her. She elbowed them aside in her rush to get to the playing field exit and once through that she ran across the hockey field and down the far bank onto the Greenacre Estate.

She looked back once, over her shoulder, at the boiler house tower that could still be seen in spite of the bank.

'Get stuffed!' she spat out before crossing the road and disappearing down a side street.

Lisa's feet ached and her suede ankle boots were saturated. Although expensive they weren't really built for rain. They were trendy though, and she had been pleased when the Carmichaels bought them for her during her first week with them. She had thought that they were different, that they cared, but the lectures and the do's and don'ts had soon become the order of the day. They were just like all the rest!

She walked and walked, oblivious of her surroundings until she recognised the little shopping centre with the bookshop and 'Albion Antiques' on the corner. It had stopped raining and a watery sun seemed to make life more bearable. There was a rainbow too, right overhead.

Lisa sighed. She knew where she was. 'Every time a winner,' she said, a wistful smile on her face. Whenever Lisa walked, lost in her own thoughts and troubles, she ended up here, far from the town centre in a quiet suburb. She knew the tracery of streets and avenues that centred on the row of shops. This was where she had grown up, started school . . . and where her world had fallen apart.

She almost turned down Beech Avenue, knowing it led to Cedar Close and the semi-detached bungalow she had shared with her mother, but instead she made for the parish church with its wishing gate and square tower. The warm rose-coloured stone glowed through the elms that circled the churchyard and here and there a few daffodils still bloomed in the pots and jars that stood on graves and monuments and grew in little clumps around the trees. On either side of the path two ancient yew trees stood to attention, like soldiers on guard, and underneath them fallen needles made a russet circle round their knotted roots.

It was a peaceful place. Lisa made for the far corner by a hawthorn hedge. It wouldn't be too long before the may blossom showered the simple stone beneath. Lisa read the stone as she did every time she came.

IN LOVING MEMORY
OF
MARGARET FISHER
Born July 1st 1955
Died December 17th 1989
Aged 34 years
GOODNIGHT MUMMY, GOD BLESS.

Lisa let the tears fall as she looked down at her mother's grave and stirred the soggy mess of last autumn's leaves with the toe of her boot.

'I'm here again, Mummy, in trouble as usual,' she cried, flopping down on the stone edging and starting to clear the leaves. Through her tears she could almost see her mother and and memories came flooding back as quickly as the tears . . .

. . . 'Lisa, Lisa! Come on, love, we'll be late!'

Lisa sat at her dressing table mirror and brushed her hair until it shone.

'I wish it was blonde and curly like Carrie's,' she grunted with effort as she attacked her straight hair with her brush.

'It suits your face just as it is,' Mrs Fisher grinned from the doorway.

Lisa swivelled on her stool and stood up.

19

'How do I look?' she asked, her small face with its cap of short brown hair tilted on one side like an inquisitive sparrow.

'You look gorgeous,' her mother said, taking both her hands and turning her around.

It was Lisa's twelfth birthday and Easter Sunday morning. It was to be a special service at church and she had new clothes for the occasion. It was the first time she had been allowed to choose her own outfit and she was feeling very pleased with herself. The skirt of her pale blue suit was short – above her knees!

Lisa felt very smart. She had chosen a white beret to match her blouse and it looked quite trendy perched on the side of her head with her fringe peeping out underneath.

'You look gorgeous too, Mummy,' she said, giving her slim dark-haired mother a hug.

'We're quite a gorgeous pair then! Look out, folks – here come the girls!' Mrs Fisher laughed, leading Lisa out of the bungalow and down the close towards the church, proud as two peacocks.

. . . It was September.

Lisa met Carrie at the corner of Bourne Road. Carrie travelled on the number 29 bus that stopped there, so Lisa always got off the school special to walk the last few hundred yards with her best friend.

Carrie was leaning on a garden wall chewing a bar of chocolate. She always had plenty of sweets in her bag and money to buy more in her pocket. Lisa's mother rationed her sweets so that she would have a healthy skin and wouldn't be fat when she was older. Lisa always did as her mother said and refused Carrie's offer of a Mars bar.

'Are you scared, Carrie?' Lisa asked.

'What of?' Carrie asked. 'We're not silly new girls!'

'I know, but it's a new year with new teachers. What if we get Miss Dodds for a form teacher! You know how I feel about her.'

'Never!' Carrie assured her. 'She always gets the GCSE lot.'

'What if we're not in the same class though?' Lisa went on. 'What if we're not together?'

Carrie pretended to stagger and reel with her hand on her brow as though her brain was hurting.

'Give me strength!' she cried. 'Lisa Fisher is brain dead. No brain, no pain! Of course we're together!'

And they were. Side by side in their desks as always, arm in arm to walk the Prison Yard as always . . . Carrie and Lisa, never spoken of singly and avowed friends for ever.

. . . It was November and Open Evening.

'Lisa is doing so well,' Mr Parks said. 'Her written work shows real promise and she's quick to answer questions. I'm expecting great things of her in the future.'

Mrs Fisher beamed at her daughter. 'She's always got her nose in a book and she spends hours on her homework,' she said.

Lisa showed her mother around the school and pointed out the pieces of work that adorned the walls of several subject rooms . . . all labelled Lisa Fisher. All the teachers nodded and smiled and Lisa felt on top of the world.

Halfway through the evening Mrs Fisher went for coffee and a chat with other parents in the canteen while Lisa, Carrie and the rest of the gang gathered by the vending machine for a Coke and a laugh. Lisa was always the centre of attention, the one with the jokes and an ability to 'take off' the teachers that had her friends in stitches. Everybody liked Lisa Fisher. She was great fun to be with.

. . . It was December and snowing as Lisa plodded up the avenue and into Cedar Close. She had stayed late to choir practice and had waited ages for a bus home. It was cold and she was tired and hungry and to add to her discomfort her bag was heavier than usual because that 'Dragon' Dodds had piled on extra homework!

The snowflakes clung to her eyelids and she tried to catch some on her tongue, almost tripping over her own feet in her efforts.

Ahead . . . through the white swirling flakes, she could just make out the flashing blue light. Something was happening at the end of the Close where it widened into a turning circle for cars.

There were people standing around.

What was happening?

There was an ambulance . . . and a police car.

Were they at her house?

Where was Mummy?

It began to rain as Lisa's tears flowed again. The grave was clear of dead leaves and flowers and the headstone revived the ache, deep inside.

'Goodnight Mummy and God bless.' . . . Those were the words Lisa had used the last time she saw her mother. She hadn't answered. Mrs Fisher had never regained consciousness after she had collapsed on the doorstep. There were packages where she had fallen, wrapped in Christmas paper and all for Lisa. The doctors said it was something called an aneurism and that there was nothing they could do even though Lisa had begged on her knees for them to make Mummy better.

No one had listened then, not the doctors, not anybody, not even God, and she had prayed so hard. She hadn't prayed since . . . not even when things were really bad. There didn't seem to be any point if you didn't get answered.

The cold gravestone penetrated her school skirt and Lisa stood up, stretching her cramped legs and wiping her face on her skirt. With swift purpose she grabbed the yellow daffodils from the next grave, jabbed them into the empty jar that leaned against her mother's headstone and left the churchyard without a backward glance, hurrying up to the terminus bus stop at the shopping centre. It wasn't difficult to cheat a bit on a full bus. She asked for a ticket to the next stop but stayed on near the back. It couldn't be done on an empty one but she rode almost all the way into town.

The pier was more crowded than usual. The amusement arcade was noisy with the sounds and jingles that came from the machines. Lisa ploughed all her money into the nearest one then kicked it as her last coin disappeared without trace.

'Oi!' a voice behind her called. 'That's not what it's for!' Lisa turned to face the scruffy looking boy that was hurrying over.

'What's it to you?' she scowled, narrowing her eyes and ready to do battle. She could feel her nails digging into her palms as the familiar angry heat began in the pit of her stomach.

'I'm in charge, doll,' he said, a lopsided grin on his spotty face. He was the sort of boy she wouldn't give a second glance to on any normal occasion . . . but this wasn't a normal occasion and he had at least noticed her! She allowed her mouth to turn up at the corners in what could loosely be called a smile.

'Kev's the name. Kevin Kershaw at your service . . . so don't kick the boxes!'

'Well! They're all fixed. You never win anything!' Lisa complained.

'How do you think the management get to spend the winter in Tenerife? Here, I'll show you. Put this 10p in.' Lisa put the money in the slot as Kev disappeared round the back of the machine and when the tumblers ground to a halt she had won 90p.

'Great stuff!' she cried, scooping the coins out of the tray. 'That's the first time I've won this much!'

'The idea is that you put it all back in!' Kev grinned.

'Not this time. It's usually 20p . . . I'm keeping this!'

'What about me? It was my 10p!'

Lisa tossed him a 10p coin and nodded when he asked if he could buy her a burger at the café on the pier. It wasn't often that somebody sought the company of Lisa Fisher. Most people avoided her as if she had chicken pox! He wasn't much to look at but he was somebody to talk to . . . and complain to. He paid for two burgers, a coffee for himself and a Coke for Lisa and she felt very grown up when he offered her a cigarette.

'Shouldn't you be in school?' he asked as he lit his and held the match for her.

Lisa waited before she answered; waited until the smoke had cleared from her mouth. Ugh! It was horrid!

'Don't go much. It's a drag,' she said, her mouth twisted in what she thought was a worldly sneer.

'Too right! I never went much either. They couldn't teach me anything. Not anything I wanted to know anyway!'

Before Kev could say anything else a hard hand grasped Lisa's shoulder and she jumped to her feet, spinning round and pushing at the figure holding her.

'Get your hands off . . .' she began, then closed her mouth with a snap as Mr Carmichael towered over her, his face far from friendly. Conscious of Kev's questioning eyebrows, Lisa took another mouthful of smoke and blew it out, slowly. An act of defiance that didn't go unnoticed.

'Put that out, Lisa, and say goodbye to your friend,' Mr Carmichael said, taking the cigarette from her and dropping it into the ashtray when she showed no sign of obeying.

'Who's the warder?' Kev asked, getting to his feet and knocking his chair over in the process.

'If I were you I would make myself scarce, young man. Feeding cigarettes to a fourteen-year-old isn't something to be proud of!' Mr Carmichael said.

'This bloke your dad?' Kev asked, backing off.

Lisa hadn't time to answer as she was marched out of the café, down the pier and out through the arcade to the promenade car park. She was too embarrassed to make a fuss, not just then anyway. People were looking and nudging each other. She had an almost uncontrollable desire to shout *Help! I'm being kidnapped!* but knew that it would only make matters worse.

Once in the car and with one eye on the granite face beside her, Lisa slumped down in her seat and put both feet up on the dashboard.

'Feet down!' Mr Carmichael said. 'You'll spoil the car.'

'I hate you and I hate your stupid car!'

'I'm not head over heels about you either, young lady,' Mr Carmichael sighed. 'You seem to thrive on trouble. Can't you see that you need a good education to get anywhere in life? Skipping school all the time will get you nowhere.'

'So what!' Lisa sulked. 'I don't want to get anywhere . . . except away from here . . . and you!'

~ 3 ~

Lisa faced Mrs Foster across the little table in the Year Tutor's room. It was a special little room designed to make people feel at ease, with low padded chairs and a coffee table. It didn't make Lisa feel at all at ease. It made her feel sick! Who did they think they were kidding with their . . . 'Let's talk about it, Lisa,' and 'I'm trying to understand, dear . . .' They could pull the other leg!

The Year Head was leaning back in her comfortable chair, her fingers pressed together in a church window arch and a sickly simpering smile on her face.

'Well, Lisa,' she said. 'We got you in this morning, which is something of an achievement!'

Lisa sat very still, her eyes fixed on the Japanese flowering cherry tree that filled the window with pink. She was aware that Mrs Foster was pretending to be friendly but didn't want any of it. They could all go and take a running jump off a cliff for all she cared – with Mrs Foster first so they could all land on her at the bottom!

'Have you nothing to say? You deliberately disobeyed me yesterday! I'm not used to girls disobeying me and I don't intend to get used to it! Are you listening?'

Lisa refused to look at Mrs Foster directly but she knew from experience that her smile had changed into a tight-lipped frown. It usually took a couple of minutes, or less.

'I really think we have to get this sorted out, Lisa, before there is serious trouble!'

How much more serious could things get!

The only sound that broke the ensuing silence was Lisa's heavy sigh of boredom and the slight rustle of her nylon ski jacket as she lifted her shoulders and let them drop again. Mrs Foster slapped both hands down on the desk.

'Lisa! If there's one thing that gets me mad it's that "I don't care" shrug of the shoulders! I think I prefer an out and out shouting match! And I won't have dumb insolence either!' she went on when there didn't seem to be any further response from Lisa.

'If it's an argument you want, you can have it right now!' Lisa said. 'And if you don't like my face . . . TOUGH!'

Mrs Foster seemed to swell in front of Lisa's eyes. The teacher was so angry she looked ready to explode and her face was red. Lisa started to giggle then laugh out loud. Mrs Foster stood up, leaning on the desk with both hands where she had banged them down.

'Right! If you won't discuss the problem of your unacceptable behaviour in a reasonable manner we shall have to take the appropriate action!'

Mrs Foster wrenched open the filing cabinet and pulled out a file of white forms.

'I'm putting you on report, Lisa. Make sure this is signed at the beginning and end of every lesson and bring it to me at the end of each day . . . until further notice, even if it takes all year!'

Lisa took the piece of paper and read the instructions.

'What's this supposed to do then?'

'It pinpoints your movements throughout the day and don't forget, it is an official document! Every time you miss a lesson your parents will be informed. There's also a place for comments on your behaviour in lessons. That will be seen by your parents too.'

'I don't have any parents.'

Mrs Foster stiffened, her lips pursed.

'You know what I mean, Lisa. Mr and Mrs Carmichael will be informed and if you persist in this attitude and behaviour you know . . .'

'I know what to expect! Is that what you were going to say? Sure I know what to expect. It's happened often enough, hasn't it? You all make certain it does!'

It meant going back into care, into another community home until another well-meaning couple took a chance on the local trouble-maker for yet another trial period. Boring!

'One place is just like another!' she muttered as she left the tutor room.

She did go to English, deciding that she'd better let things cool down a bit. She wasn't giving in exactly, just taking a little rest.

'Well I never!' Mr Simpson gasped in mock horror when Lisa appeared for Science, 'To what do we owe this high honour, Miss Fisher? Is this the second time you've graced us with your presence this term or is it the third?'

When Lisa didn't answer his sarcastic remarks he got quite angry.

'You hear this, madam! I'm not having my lesson ruined by your disruptive behaviour. I know all about you! You're the only topic of conversation in the staff room. You can sit at the back and read something, I don't care what! I don't want to know you're there! You're so far behind you'll never catch up with the work . . . and I'm not entering you for the exam!'

Someone sniggered as Lisa had her report signed and moved to the back of the lab.

She didn't go to Maths, locking herself in a toilet for the whole of the lesson and writing on the walls in felt tip.

SCHOOL STINKS she wrote in letters three inches high then she tore the report into little pieces and flushed it down the toilet.

When Lisa arrived for RE, Mrs Harris was busy setting up the TV and video player.

'Hello, Lisa. You're nice and early!' she said cheerfully. 'Could you pop some chairs into a circle for me while I find the place on this tape?'

Lisa liked Mrs Harris. There weren't many girls who didn't. It was probably because most of her lessons were talks and discussion, not a lot of writing, and were often funny. She told them things about herself and her family. They had problems too and it helped to sort things out when people shared their feelings and hopes. She always listened and didn't judge people from what others said and, most important, she made you think for yourself and sort out how you felt about things.

Mrs Harris had four children, two boys and two girls. One of her boys had been in trouble with the police, for stealing, but she was not afraid to use his problems as an example to make a point, and her eldest daughter had left home after a family argument.

Mrs Harris admitted the mistakes she had made in handling her children and suggested how she should have reacted.

Mrs Harris told things as they were.

Lisa watched the video with more attention than she had given to anything for a long time. It was all about belief and a class of small children talked about God and Jesus. One little boy described God as being kind, like a father, Lisa thought about fathers. The only one she knew anything about had left her when she was three and she didn't want to think about the last time she'd seen him. He certainly wasn't kind.

The biggest part of the documentary was about the Holy Land, especially Jerusalem, and discussed many of the places mentioned in the Gospels and the happenings that form the basis of Christian faith.

Lisa felt a lump rising in her throat when the voice talked about the resurrection and life after death. She felt the tears gathering and so, to cover up her feelings and retain her hard image, she attacked.

'Rubbish!' she said, loudly enough to turn heads.

Mrs Harris didn't react at all but waited until the video ended with a shot of a lonely cave on a hillside. Then she turned to the class. They were sitting in a semi-circle ready for the discussion that everybody enjoyed, even Lisa.

'Right, Lisa, let's hear it. Why is the resurrection story rubbish . . . according to you?'

Lisa gulped. She did enjoy the discussions but usually listened. Mrs Harris was trying to make her lead the talk!

'It just is . . . rubbish!' she said.

'Come now, Lisa. That's just an easy get-out. If you make a statement like that the least you can do is qualify it, give your reasons. That's the only way I'll accept an opinion. Out with it! Say what you mean. The floor is yours . . . and the chair . . . and all our ears, most of them.'

The girls giggled and Lisa grinned. Mrs Harris always made her feel better but she wasn't sure she could explain what she meant.

'I don't believe it,' she began. 'Nobody's ever come back to tell us what happens when we die. There's no proof. People just die and that's the end of it. There isn't anything else after this.'

'What about those people who stop breathing on

operating tables? I've read about them in a book my dad got from a book club. They say they go down a tunnel with a bright light at the end but something fetches them back and they come back to life!' Samantha Jameson said.

'Dreams . . . imagination. People see what they want to see,' Lisa mumbled.

'Jesus died and rose again,' Tracy butted in. 'Everybody knows that!'

'Not everybody, Tracy,' Mrs Harris said. 'It is the basis of the Christian faith. There are many people in the world, and in this country, who believe differently.'

'I don't see why Jesus had to die at all. God is supposed to love everybody yet he let his son die,' Lisa said, thinking about her mother.

Mrs Harris tried to make Lisa say what she was thinking.

'Why do you think God doesn't love everybody?'

'Because my mother loved him . . . and she died.'

There. It was out. Lisa waited for the mumbling comments but the class were silent.

'It says in the Bible that Jesus' blood would be given for many for the forgiveness of sins. My mother never sinned. She didn't need to be forgiven for anything. She was always kind to everybody and never hurt anybody. It wasn't fair . . . was it?'

Mrs Harris leaned forward, aware of all the class but her eyes on Lisa.

'Jesus taught that God is love, and loves us in spite of the wrongs we do. And we all do them, all of us!'

Lisa and several others started to protest but Mrs Harris held up her hand. She hadn't finished.

'Come on, Lisa, be honest. Haven't you skipped the odd lesson or two? Taken a biscuit or an apple without asking? Said, or even thought, something unkind that would hurt? Let's have a show of hands. Who can honestly say that they've never . . . ever . . . taken something that didn't belong to them?'

One or two hands were half raised but were lowered again as a remembered pencil or rubber caused a blush.

'Who has never said an unkind word? Called somebody a name that was far from complimentary? Told a tall tale? Told a lie?' The girls were silent, uncomfortable, and for once Lisa felt at one with the class.

'God can't overlook our naughty little ways,' Mrs Harris said, wagging her finger from side to side and making them smile. 'Things must be made right just as they are when people break our civil laws and are punished. God gave his son for the sins of the world and to prove his forgiveness.'

'But that has nothing to do with living and dying,' Lisa commented. 'My mother isn't here with me now, like people say Jesus is!'

'It's eternal life in heaven, isn't it, Mrs Harris?' a girl at the back of the room said.

'I don't believe in heaven either,' Lisa said. 'We can't see it or touch it. It's just talk.'

'What *do* you believe?' Mrs Harris asked.

Lisa thought hard, trying to put her thoughts into sensible words.

'I believe that I have to look after myself, because nobody else will.'

'Many people believe that Jesus looks after them. It makes a difference to the way they live and the way they treat others. They are sure of God's love,' Mrs Harris said.

'Jesus wasn't. He thought God, his father, had abandoned him, didn't he?' Lisa asked.

Mrs Harris was surprised that Lisa knew as much as she did. She had not shown so much interest before!

'I think he was experiencing what it is like to be no longer friends with God, to lose one's way and be separated from him. Jesus was taking the punishment for others. As a result, everyone who believes and depends on him rather than themselves can be forgiven. They enter God's kingdom and become friends with him for ever.'

Just then the buzzer sounded for the end of lesson and lunch-time. Lisa was quite sorry the morning had gone. It was the first one she had enjoyed for a long time. The discussion had made her think, something she hadn't done much of lately, except to moan about how miserable she was.

For once she hung about instead of dashing off. 'Do *you* believe that there's a heaven and that God loves everybody?' she asked Mrs Harris when the rest of the class had gone.

Mrs Harris paused at her desk, collecting her handbag and file to take to the staffroom. 'What I believe is not the issue, Lisa. What *you* believe is important.'

'I don't know. I'm not sure,' Lisa mumbled as she shuffled to the door.

Mrs Harris put her hand on Lisa's shoulder as they left the room together. Lisa was about to shrug it off and snap 'get lost!' – her usual reaction, but she paused. It was a firm hand and somehow reassuring.

'Try talking to Jesus about it. You've started talking to me so it shouldn't be too difficult. He listens too, you know!' Mrs Harris said with a smile as they parted company.

Lisa managed to get to the dining room without a confrontation with one of her enemies. She felt quite good and a lot less miserable than before the RE lesson.

It didn't last long! In Lisa's life the good moments were few, and short lived!

Carrie Rogers, surrounded as always by her backing group, deliberately knocked Lisa's beaker of water all over the vegetable lasagne she had just paid 85p for at the serving hatch. It was impossible to contain herself.

'You stupid cow!' she shrieked, jumping to her feet.

Over went the chair, several small fry and their trays as Lisa went for Carrie, who was saved, fortunately, by two dinner ladies – one holding Lisa and one standing between her and her enemy.

'What's to do?' Mrs Black asked, letting Lisa go.

'Look what she's done. That's my dinner gone!' Lisa shouted.

'It was an accident, stupid!' Carrie yelled back.

'Accident my foot. You'd better pay up or I'll . . .'

'You'll what, Fishface? Get lost!'

'That's quite enough!'

The voice was loud and recognisably authoritative. It was Mrs Foster.

'You again Lisa Fisher . . . !' she began.

'But . . .' Lisa tried to explain.

'No buts, out!' Mrs Foster ordered. 'And wait outside my room!' The two girls left the dining room together, red-faced as all the younger girls nudged each other and whispered in the hush that followed the outburst.

'What's the use!' Lisa growled.

Carrie went to Mrs Foster's room, Lisa didn't! Instead she made for the cloakroom and rifled all the coat pockets along a row of pegs.

'32p! Better than nothing!' she said between clenched teeth. This time she left via the science block door that led across the back of the car park and round by the sports hall. There were plenty of girls about but nobody stopped her or spoke to her.

'Or even care if I live or die!' she thought. On impulse she popped into the sports hall and jabbed at the fire alarm with her thumb. The thin glass broke and the resulting siren wailed behind her as she ran for the gate and made for the promenade.

'That'll show them!'

Kev was working on the pier again. Lisa felt her heart lift a little when she saw him. He wasn't up to much but at least he looked pleased to see her.

'Hi!' he grinned. 'Wagging it again?'

'Bet you did when you were at school!'

'Me? Never . . . Well, maybe once or twice . . . a week!'

They both laughed and Lisa told him about Carrie and her dinner and about setting off the fire alarm.

'So nobody's getting any dinner!' Kev said with a grin. 'That was always one of my best tricks, a great way to miss a boring lesson – unless it was raining! I never liked standing about in the rain. Come on, let's get a burger. Can't have you dying of starvation.'

For a brief moment Lisa felt angry with him. She was going to suggest that he read the papers or watched the TV news before he made jokes about starvation but she knew the comment would be lost on him. He wasn't the sort to care about such things.

'Did they ever catch you?' Lisa asked as they ate their lunch at the café on the pier. It seemed the only thing he could talk about – knocking school and authority, so Lisa prompted him to fill the embarrassing silences.

'No way! I'm too smart. I got away with murder!'

It was Kev's lunch hour so they went to the shopping precinct in the town centre.

'I need some fags, hang about a bit,' he said as they strolled through one of the big department stores.

When he came back from the kiosk Lisa was looking at a little diary bound in red leather.

'Isn't this nice?' she said, turning the pages to show him the quality of the paper and the gold edging. 'There's a whole page for each day and a wild flower printed in each corner.'

'Have it if you fancy it,' Kev said, standing close behind her.

'I've only got about 40p. It's £3.50!' Lisa whispered loudly. She was a bit embarrassed. She didn't want him to think she was asking him to buy it for her!

'I didn't say buy it. I said have it, take it!'

Lisa froze, the diary clutched in her hand. 'I can't. I daren't!'

'Sure you can, it's simple. Pop it up your sleeve, it's small enough. I get most of my stuff that way.'

Lisa gulped. 'What if I get caught?'

'Never! Nobody's looking. Go on, do it now, I'm shielding you!' Kev urged.

Lisa slipped the diary inside her sleeve where the ribbed cuff of her ski jacket held it securely.

'I've done it, let's go,' she whispered.

'Let's not!' Kev answered, taking her arm. 'Let's look round the store.'

Lisa had a large lump in her throat as they strolled through the store, picking up this and that and listening to the music at the tape counter. Kev even asked one of the supervisors where the stationery department was, then he bought two packets of crisps and paid for them at the cash desk before they walked out, munching and giggling.

It was all so easy!

~ 4 ~

Friday was a bad day.

It started as soon as she woke up, with Mrs Carmichael insisting she wore the proper school jumper. Lisa preferred her sweatshirt but her foster mother wouldn't hear of it. She stood there, with her face all red and shiny and her permed hair laquered into stiff curls, waving the knitted jumper in the air.

'Uniform is uniform, Lisa, and this is it! Now don't make life difficult . . . put it on.'

There was no way she could ever call Mrs Carmichael Mom! Not ever! Her own mother would have let her wear the sweatshirt. Her own mother was always on her side!

Then, at breakfast, Mr Carmichael went on and on about school and GCSEs, careers and getting the right qualifications.

'You have a serious attitude problem, my girl,' he said, with his mouth full of cornflakes. 'You don't try to be pleasant. You think the world owes you a living! You have to work for what you get, believe me! I never had things handed to me on a plate. You young people don't know what work is! I had to pull out all the stops to get where I am. Mom will tell you how hard I've worked. I got the exams I needed . . . you have to have those or you're nobody, nothing! Tell her, Mom!'

Lisa groaned. Did he *have* to use that stupid name? He sounded like a stupid American! Boring! Boring! Boring!

Luckily for her he was so wrapped up in himself and how hard he worked he didn't hear the groan and Lisa escaped without another row. Then she missed the bus and that made her late, putting her name in the late book again and adding an adverse comment to her class attendance report.

Then at ten o'clock she was pulled out of a lesson and taken to the tutor room. It was impossible to run off because the secretary who fetched her walked so close she would have had to step on her to get past! She fully expected to find Mrs Foster scowling from the easy chair and yet another report form ready on the desk, but there was a stranger sitting there.

The woman was tall, fair and quite nice looking. Lisa guessed that she was about thirty-five. She wasn't wearing a wedding ring.

'Let me explain who I am,' she began, closing the file in front of her and clasping her hands, loosely.

Lisa didn't wait for explanations. 'Is that about me?' she said, eyeing the file suspiciously.

'Not really. Some of it has some relevance to your case.'

Her case? What was all this about?

'What does that mean . . . my case? You make me sound mental or something. Nobody's going to put me away!'

'Nobody is going to put you anywhere, Lisa. It's nothing like that. You've been referred to the School Support Team, the S.S.T. Have you heard of it? No? Well, my name is Joy Taylor and I've been assigned to . . .'

'Has that cow Foster sent for you? It's her that wants putting away. She's always picking on me!' Lisa said angrily.

'Nobody sent for me, Lisa, and nobody's getting at you. It came out at a staff meeting that you're having trouble . . . unhappy . . . under-achieving . . . feeling persecuted. Am I making any sense?'

'They should all mind their own business!' Lisa growled, folding her arms and slumping down into the chair with her feet up on the coffee table.

Miss Taylor didn't tell her to take them down!

'It *is* their business Lisa. The teachers just want you to reach your potential, to achieve what you're capable of. They are just doing their job.'

'I heard all about jobs at breakfast this morning, thank you,' Lisa said, taking a piece of gum out of its wrapper and popping it into her mouth.

Miss Taylor didn't tell her to put it in the bin!

'The staff who teach you are really concerned about . . .'

'Rubbish!' Lisa snapped, letting her feet fall off the table with a bump that jarred her whole body. 'You can't fool me! All they do is complain and pick on me for nothing!'

'What about the truancy? Isn't that something to complain about? You are missing vital work in a very important year. And apart from that, several parents have complained about disruption in lessons and that is quite serious. You could be excluded for good, you know. Nobody wants that . . . not even Mrs Foster. Oh, I know . . .' she went on when Lisa started to protest, 'You don't exactly hit it off with Mrs Foster but you don't help the situation, do you?'

Lisa was silent.

Miss Taylor waited for what seemed ages then carried on. 'I'm not here to punish or complain, Lisa. I'm here to help, to counsel you . . . to listen to what you have to say.'

'You'll be the first that has!' Lisa muttered.

'Good. Then I'll be the first. Where would you like to begin?'

Lisa bit her lip. This was a new approach.

'I just ask one small thing, though. I'm not shouting, using bad language or calling you names. Do you think you could offer me the same courtesy, Lisa?'

'Why should anybody bother with me? What's in it for you? I'm nobody . . . worth nothing!' Lisa began, her voice starting to break and her eyes tingling like they do when tears are not far away.

'Did someone tell you that, or are you making an assumption because things are not just to your liking at the moment? Everyone has something about them that is of worth,' Miss Taylor said softly.

'I don't think I have,' Lisa whispered.

Miss Taylor was so nice and comfortable to be with that Lisa found herself relaxing in the chair. Miss Taylor posed no threat, Lisa found her hands unclenching slowly and looked at the red half-moons where her nails had dug into her palms. It was like talking to herself . . . in a mirror.

Once Lisa had begun . . . at the beginning . . . it was easy to pour out all the hurt . . .

. . . It was raining heavily and the white snow had melted into grey mush. Lisa wondered why it always rained at funerals. All the films she'd seen had rainy funerals or the graveyards were thick with fog.

She watched the coffin being lowered into the grave. There was muddy water at the bottom and muddy footsteps on the plastic grass at the sides. Only a few mourners stood in the corner of the churchyard for there wasn't any family that she knew of. A friend of her mother's cried softly into a white hanky and two women from the social services stood on either side of her. There were people on the edge of her vision but they were putting flowers on another grave. Lisa dropped a paper flower onto the coffin as it disappeared. She had made it herself from Christmas wrapping paper, gold paper that had wrapped the little box with a cross and chain in it, one of her presents.

When it was over, Lisa was left alone for a few brief moments then whisked away in a car with nothing but a small suitcase.

The nights she spent crying in a children's home were little more than a blur. Then came the long train journey with one of the women who had been at the funeral.

'Your father has agreed to take you, Lisa, on trial. So be a good girl, won't you? He's married again and has a new family. It's very kind of him to make you a part of it. You're going to be really happy, Lisa. You will be a good girl, won't you?'

Lisa looked out of the train window at the grey sky and the grey world. The trees were empty; the blank windows of tower blocks and bungalows were empty and Lisa Fisher was as empty as the landscape the train hurried through.

The city was big and noisy and they had to travel on the underground to where her father lived. Lisa didn't enjoy it at all. The tunnels were long and dark and people ran up and down the escalators instead of standing holding the rails as it said. She was frightened of falling and getting pulled into the grids and mangled up. The trains made a lot of noise and Lisa was glad when they emerged into the fresh air again.

She couldn't remember her father clearly and didn't recognise Mr Fisher when he opened the door. There hadn't been any photographs of him at home.

'Well, Mr Fisher, here we are. This is Lisa,' the social

worker said, pushing Lisa through the doorway. 'It's been a long journey.'

'I suppose you'd better come in,' he grumbled. 'But bear in mind that it's not definitely a permanent arrangement!'

The flat was small and Lisa had to share a bedroom with two little boys. They were twins and about eighteen months old. They weren't attractive little boys. They had light carroty hair and dirty faces and one of them had a snotty nose. There was a nasty stale smell in the flat too.

Mr Fisher had a wife called Lynne who was very young and spoke with a funny accent. She hardly spoke to Lisa at all, which was a good thing because Lisa couldn't tell what she said.

By the time she had put her few belongings in the one drawer she was allowed, the social worker had gone and Lisa was left alone in the bedroom. She sat on the single bed with its none too clean duvet and waited for something to happen. She wasn't sure what she was supposed to do.

'Don't you want any dinner?' Lynne said from the hallway outside the bedroom door.

Lisa shook her head.

'Suit yerself!'

She could smell fish and chips and felt empty inside but she didn't want to go into the living room.

When the family had eaten, the two little boys were put in their cots. One of them cried continuously and there was a terrible smell coming from somewhere. Both boys were in nappies and Lisa could see that the fatter one had filled his and was uncomfortable.

'Get to bed then,' Lynne said. 'We're off out for an hour so you watch Darrel and Jason for me, can't you. It's nice to have a baby-sitter. They cost a fortune round here!'

As they went out of the door Bob Fisher paused. 'There's no room for you here, not really. It's only a trial. If you're a help to Lynne and she don't mind . . . well . . . we'll see. There's biscuits and bread if you're hungry, but don't go rooting about in things that don't concern you!' he said.

Lisa stayed in the bedroom. Darrel, or Jason went on crying and after a while Lisa joined him until they both fell asleep.

Days came and went. Lisa didn't know whether it was Sunday or Wednesday. Mr Fisher went out at seven in the morning and came back at seven at night. Nothing was mentioned about school and Lisa never left the flat. Most of her time was spent looking after the boys while Lynne popped out, which she seemed to do all the time, for a long time. She seemed to do a lot of shopping but there was never anything to eat in the place. Lisa had to wash up after supper. It was the only meal they got and mostly from the take-away; fish, steak pie or sausage and chips for Mr Fisher and Lynne and just chips on a paper for the children. They had chips every night and sometimes a slice of bread and butter, if Lynne remembered to buy bread.

During the day they ate biscuits, cornflakes, chocolate or bread and something . . . whatever Lisa could find. At least there was milk! That was delivered each morning and Lisa got up before Lynne to make sure that at least one bottle was hidden for Darrel and Jason.

Lisa stopped eating but no-one noticed.

Late one night Lisa woke up to the sound of raised voices and breaking crockery. Darrel and Jason started screaming and wailing and Lisa was terrified. It was something new to her, having lived nearly all her life with just a mother, and a quiet, kind and gentle mother too.

In spite of her own fears she tried to comfort the twins.

It wasn't their fault they had awful parents. She put both of them into her bed, one on each side of her and cuddled them, stroking their backs and making soothing noises. The last thing she wanted was her father coming in, she was sure he would hit them if he did. Lisa had never heard people shout at each other.

'You're a lazy bitch!' Bob Fisher was shouting. 'Look at this place, it's like a pig sty! What the 'ell do you do all day, sit on your backside?'

'You don't have to cope with three kids! You're out and about, meeting people and having a laugh . . . I'm stuck here all day with this lot. It isn't my idea of fun, watching them three eat and sleep and make a mess! And one of them isn't even mine!' Lynne complained.

'She's not *mine* either!' Bob yelled.

Lisa went cold. What did he mean?

She put the boys back in their cots and left them whimpering while she went to stand at the living room door.

It was open, just a little way, and she could see broken plates on the floor and food on the wall. Lynne was crouching on the floor and her lip was bleeding.

'What do you mean she's not yours?' she sniffed.

'Margaret was as bad as you . . . no idea about running a decent home. She was always gadding about, with women friends, she said, but who was she kidding? I was away a lot, looking for work. When I was working I was away weeks at a time . . . driving. Who knows what she was up to? I never took to the kid, she means nothing to me and I don't want her here. She means nothing to me . . . she doesn't even look like me!'

Lisa couldn't help the cry that escaped from her mouth and it made Bob Fisher lurch towards the door.

'What the . . . ?'

He flung the door wide and glared at Lisa. She could smell drink on his breath and was terrified.

'Spying are you? We'll soon put a stop to that!' he shouted. 'Get back to bed and shut those brats up before I smash their heads in!'

'You leave my boys alone, Bob Fisher, or I'll. . . .'

'You'll what?' Bob sneered. 'They don't look like me either so watch what you say, woman.'

Lisa couldn't move. Her legs felt like lead and she was shaking so much that her teeth chattered.

'Move, I said!' he growled at her and at the same time he hit her on the side of her head with the back of his hand.

'Pack her bags . . . she's not wanted here . . . !'

' . . . And what happened then, Lisa?' Miss Taylor asked, very quietly.

Lisa found it difficult to tell her any more but she tried. She told her about the first children's home, about misery and rejection and how her behaviour got worse; about the various foster homes where she couldn't settle, about her temper and the awful feeling of worthlessness, of not belonging; about the Carmichaels not understanding and getting at her all the time and then the buzzer went and the session ended.

Miss Taylor asked if she would like to talk again and Lisa shrugged as she nodded.

Once outside in the corridor she began to shake. She tried hard to stop but couldn't. Talking so much about that visit to her father's home had brought all her buried memories back into her thoughts. She hadn't told Miss Taylor everything. She hadn't mentioned the belt that he beat her with or the kicks with his boot. Nobody knew about that or about the terrible things he called her . . . and her mother. No-one would hurt her like that again.

'No one will get that close!' she muttered, angry at

having said as much as she had, and crying with that anger.

She rounded a corner and ran straight into Mrs Harris. 'Whatever is the matter, Lisa?'

The kind voice and concerned look on Mrs Harris' face turned Lisa's anger to misery. Anyone else would have yelled at her and demanded to know where she was going and why she was out of lessons. It really did seem as though Mrs Harris was interested in her, and cared.

'What is it love, somebody upset you?'

Lisa just shook her head, the tears really falling.

'In here, quick,' Mrs Harris said, opening the library door with her keys. 'It's not in use this lesson.'

Once inside and away from prying eyes, Mrs Harris put both arms around Lisa and let her cry, just standing quietly until she was calm enough to speak.

'I'm sorry that I bumped into you,' she said.

'It's not important, Lisa, but you are! Can you tell me about it?'

Lisa shook her head. She didn't think she could, not yet.

'Try . . . a trouble shared is like a shopping bag with two handles, it's nice when two can share the weight,' Mrs Harris said, giving her a hug. 'The trouble is, when I walk with my eldest daughter I seem to take all the weight. I've got shorter arms you see!'

Lisa found her mouth turning up at the corners in spite of her misery.

'I could do with a bag with one long handle and one short one. That would even things up a bit. Ah! A smidgin of a smile. That's better,' Mrs Harris said as she fumbled in her bag for a tissue. 'So what's the matter?'

'Nothing really. I've just been seeing a counsellor and it brought back memories,' Lisa sighed, wiping her eyes.

'Too painful to share?'

Lisa nodded but frowned. She was puzzled.

'I've never told anyone what I told that Miss Taylor. I wonder why I told her?'

'Sometimes it's better to talk to somebody you're not close to or involved with. That's why psychiatrists make so much money. Zey 'ave vays of makink you talk!'

Lisa grinned. 'Perhaps that's what I should be when I leave school. Someone people can talk to, like Miss Taylor and you,' she said.

Mrs Harris picked up the pile of books she had dumped on the library desk.

'There is somebody that everyone can talk to whenever they feel the need, you know. Jesus always listens and sometimes the answers to our most difficult problems become clear. Why don't you talk to him?'

'I don't think I believe anything, so why would he listen to me?'

'Try him. I think you'll be surprised,' Mrs Harris said. 'I have to go, Lisa . . . I'm teaching now and I'm late. I hope they haven't murdered each other in my absence!'

Lisa lay very still under her duvet. The room was dark but for the light of the street lamp that filtered through the loosely woven curtains at her window.

She listened. A car sped along the ring road with that peculiar sound that Mr Carmichael had told her was the 'Doppler Effect' . . . faint as it comes near, then loud, then shifting to a lower key as it passed and fading into nothing into the distance. Somewhere close by a milk bottle fell down stone steps, probably knocked over by a cat on the prowl. Someone called goodnight and a door slammed after footsteps had run down a garden path.

Downstairs the constant buzz of the television was punctuated by the odd comment and the clattering of coffee cups.

Mr and Mrs Carmichael weren't so bad . . . at a distance!

Lisa tried talking to Jesus as Mrs Harris had suggested.

'Why is everybody at me all the time? They never leave me alone. Why do people hate me? Why can't I make friends? What have I done so wrong that I'm being punished?' she whispered to her pillow. There was no immediate answer but gradually a quiet voice inside her head began to answer some of her questions . . . answers she didn't like. She tried to think of other, more pleasant things but the truth would out . . .

You don't . . . do your work, try to be pleasant, accept criticism, ask for help, admit you're wrong!

You are . . . rude to people, disruptive in class, bad tempered and loud-mouthed, incapable of keeping a friend.

You do . . . skip lessons, skip school, thumb your nose at authority, steal money and bully young girls.

A dozen other reasons for her unhappiness came to mind and Lisa knew she was her own worst enemy.

'You know where you're going wrong, Lisa Fisher!' she said aloud. 'You get what you give . . . *nothing!*'

Then, as the tears began to fall she added, very softly, 'Help me. Oh please help me.'

~ 5 ~

Lisa managed to stay in school for the rest of the week and stay out of trouble.

'This homework is quite reasonable!' Miss Dodds remarked with some surprise. 'Are you sure it's your own work?'

Lisa bit her tongue, wanting so much to put Doddy in her place, but she didn't. She kept her temper.

'Yes, Miss Dodds,' she said aloud, while inside her head she was shouting . . . 'They don't believe it when I'm good! I can't win whatever I do!'

Miss Dodds collapsed in her chair, in a mock fainting fit, causing the class to giggle but Lisa still kept her cool. Maybe Jesus hadn't answered her yet but she'd sorted some things out for herself, and one of them was to keep her head and close her mouth!

All in all it wasn't a bad couple of days. On Saturday she had a lie-in, a luxury allowed at the weekend, and didn't surface until almost ten-thirty when the smell of frying bacon set her taste buds in action.

'Good morning, Lisa,' Mrs Carmichael said brightly. 'Had a good sleep? Say hello to Jamey!'

Sitting in the old high chair was a very small child.

'Jamey who?' Lisa asked, taking the little boy's hand and shaking it.

'Just Jamey. He's come to stay for a while. He needs a home and some love just now.'

Don't we all? Lisa said to herself, then felt uncomfortable. The Carmichaels were quite nice, really.

'Jamey is two and a bit, but he's so small we've had to get the baby chair out of the loft so that he can sit with us at the table. Haven't we, Jamey?' Mrs Carmichael said, ruffling his blonde curls as she passed him to put bread in the toaster. 'Do you want some bacon Lisa?'

'No thanks, I'll just have some toast after this.'

Lisa watched Jamey as she ate her cereal. He was very quiet, not at all like Darrel and Jason who had done nothing but whine all day. They were bigger than him too, she remembered. He had the bluest of blue eyes and they were studying her as hard as she was studying him.

'He's finished, so he can come out if he wants,' Mrs Carmichael said, as she buttered toast.

'Do you want to come out?' Lisa asked, holding out her arms to him.

At first Jamey sat quite still, staring at Lisa as if he didn't understand, then he tried to back away through the chair, as if terrified of her.

'Whatever's the matter with him?' she asked.

'He's had a bit of a rough time, Lisa. He's afraid of us, of everybody. We'll have to win him over, convince him we're nice people. It may take a lot of time and patience before he trusts us.'

Lisa held out her arms again, and smiled. Very softly she called his name.

'Jamey. Come to Lisa, Jamey.'

Slowly his little arms stretched out to her.

Something happened. It was as if somebody had pressed a switch and released a tide. Lisa felt it rise and fall inside her until it almost spilled out as tears when

Jamey's arms curled tightly round her neck and held her so tightly she could hardly breathe. Then his cheek touched hers . . . magic!

'He's so thin, Mum!' she whispered.

Mrs Carmichael almost dropped the butter knife. It was the first time Lisa had called her anything, much less Mum . . . and a little unexpected!

'He is, Lisa, and it's up to us to make him into the chubby little man he should be . . . and one that smiles. I shall need help, if you've the time?'

It was then, as she sat down for her toast with Jamey on her knee, that she noticed the purple bruise on his leg, the long scratch on his arm and the bump on the back of his head.

'Somebody's been hitting him!' she gasped.

Memories of a belt, a clenched fist and a heavy boot swam before Lisa's eyes for the second time that week. She remembered how scared she had been with her father towering over her, and how helpless against the blows. Jamey was so little he must have been terrified. She gave him a hug.

'There's a good boy,' she said, giving him a finger of buttery toast. 'Lisa will keep you safe.'

He ate, keeping his eyes on Lisa all the time and managed the tiniest of smiles. It made Lisa feel special.

'What happened to him?' she asked.

'We don't know . . . and it isn't really our business, Lisa. Our job is to love him and take care of him, for a while.'

'A long while?'

'Who knows,' Mrs Carmichael sighed. 'Sometimes a week, sometimes ten years!'

Lisa gave him another hug and another toast finger.

'Say Lisa, Jamey,' she coaxed. 'Lisa!'

Jamey tried but all he managed was 'Eetha' in a tiny high voice.

'That's the first squeak we've had out of that little mouse all morning!' Mrs Carmichael laughed.

'When did he arrive?' Lisa asked, wiping the butter from his chin with a paper hanky.

'About half past four this morning. He needed someone urgently, as you can see. That's why we're foster parents, Pop and me. We're always here for children who need us, just like Jamey . . . and you.'

Lisa was just about to say 'I don't need anybody' but stopped herself just in time. She did need a roof over her head and anything was better than The Grange where she had found herself after her trip to London. She had slept in a room with five other girls. Within days they had taken her cross and chain, laughed when she cried and played the innocent victims when she fought back with a rolling pin.

Mr and Mrs Carmichael had given her a home, quite a nice one, in spite of her bad record and they did look after her. That they looked after her a bit too much was her own opinion!

Two previous sets of foster parents had given up at the first sign of trouble and a third after she had wrecked a bedroom in a quarrel with another girl. Up to now she had been the only one at the Carmichaels and hadn't thought about them fostering other children.

Let's face it . . . I haven't given them much thought at all, she said to herself.

'Do you mind if we put him in with you for the time being? I don't think he'll be happy in the little bedroom on his own. He needs company just now, somebody he trusts. You seem to fit that bill, Lisa,' Mrs Carmichael said.

Lisa didn't mind at all and helped move the top half of the spare room bunks into her own room.

Lisa and Mrs Carmichael chattered like best friends as they re-arranged the room to take Jamey's little bed, moving hers right under the window.

'Are you sure it won't be too draughty?' Mrs Carmichael asked, looking round the room.

'It will be lovely on summer mornings,' Lisa said with a smile.

Lisa discovered that in twenty years the Carmichaels had fostered fifty-three children, most of them short-term and in need of a safe haven, some new babies awaiting adoption and a few who had stayed for a longer period.

'How short is short-term?' Lisa asked.

'Sometimes overnight, sometimes a week or two or even more if it's a baby up for adoption.'

'Isn't it hard to give babies back when you've loved them?'

'Yes, but most short-stay children come to us because their mums are sick and are in hospital. It's rewarding to help people, and besides, look what we get!' Mrs Carmichael picked up Jamey, gave him a cuddle and settled him in his newly made bed. 'A little cherub like this to love for a while.'

Lisa couldn't help thinking that they got people like her too, who brought nothing but trouble with them!'

'Who stayed the longest?' she asked, not wanting the conversation to end.

'That would be Jennifer, I think. She came to us when her parents – and grandparents – died in a car crash. She was seven then.'

Mrs Carmichael paused, as if remembering something nice. 'She got married from here,' she said. 'A lovely wedding that Pop and I helped her with. She was just twenty, and very much in love with her Robert. There's an album downstairs. Would you like to see?'

Lisa nodded. It was strange, almost as if Mrs Carmichael was talking about her own daughter.

Jamey had snuggled down in his bed. He had fallen

asleep, probably exhausted after his eventful night.

Lisa gazed at his sleeping face. He had his hand under his cheeks as he lay on the pale blue pillow.

'He looks like a little angel,' Lisa whispered.

'So did you when you arrived, with your pale blue suit and big blue eyes!' There was a little smile on Mrs Carmichael's face, a lopsided smile, as if to say . . . What happened?

Lisa blushed. She had been a bit of a pain! They sat together on the settee, leaving the lounge door open so that they would hear the little boy if he woke up, and leafed through two big photo albums. Every picture was of this child or that. Marie at the fair, Paul on his first bike, Laura and her teddy and pages more.

There was a whole section devoted to tiny babies who all looked alike to Lisa but Mrs Carmichael named every one and had something nice to say about them all.

'And here are those I call my sons and daughters, Lisa. These are the long stays . . . like Jennifer. You haven't met her yet. She comes to see us twice a year. They met at college you see, and Robert is Scottish. They live in Edinburgh where Robert is a teacher and Jennifer is mother to Simon and Emma, who are twins. Here they are!'

There were photos of Jennifer at seven, ten, thirteen, sixteen, nineteen and on her wedding day. The last picture was of the family. Jennifer and Robert holding both babies, one in each arm. Someone had written 'To Grandma and Grandpa from Simon and Emma.'

'He's very . . .' Lisa began.

'Dishy? I'll say he is. Jennifer was in love the first time she clapped eyes on him. Look at my grandchildren. Aren't they *gorgeous*?'

Lisa was very puzzled. Mrs Carmichael really thought of Jennifer as her daughter. She really loved her, she could see that.

'And this is Matthew. You'll be meeting him shortly. He's in the Air Force and comes home when he can. He's been in Germany for a year and is due some leave. That's another reason for wanting Jamey in with you. Matthew will need the spare bed when he comes. You've got his bedroom now. He'll probably scare Jamey. He's a big lad, as you can see.'

'Won't he want his own bedroom back?' Lisa asked.

'Bless you no! He's not 'in care' any more. He's nearly twenty and doesn't live here, officially. But he still looks on Pop and me as his parents and this as his home. He came to us when he was eleven. Here he is, a little terror and nothing but trouble!'

'All these children,' Lisa sighed as she examined the photographs.

'They weren't all angels. We've had our troubles too . . . it's been hard work sometimes.'

'But you get paid for having us, don't you?' Lisa wished she hadn't said that. Mrs Carmichael's face changed. She looked very sad and hurt.

'I didn't mean . . .'

'That's all right, Lisa, you're right. We do get paid to look after you, until you are seventeen and old enough to take care of yourselves. We can ask you to leave then . . . that's the law.'

Mrs Carmichael closed the albums and stood up.

'I'd better get on with the washing up before Jamey wakes up. There's some shopping to do when Pop gets back. You can come if you want, and help with Jamey,' she said.

Lisa would have liked to look at the last pages in the album, to see if she was there, but they were safely back in the cupboard again.

'Why can't I keep my mouth shut?' she muttered angrily.

After lunch they went shopping. It was difficult to park in the centre of town and the car parks were always full on market days. The bus to the centre stopped just down the road from the house so it was easier to take that.

'We'd better make for the bank first, if this little chap needs clothes and shoes. I hope the cash machine isn't empty,' Mr Carmichael said as they got off the bus at the station.

'We could use a cheque!' Mrs Carmichael suggested.

'Every transaction costs money . . . I don't use a cheque if I can help it!'

Lisa felt her mouth turn down into what was the beginning of a sneer. Wasn't that just like him . . . taking everything so carefully and seriously? Silly old . . . !

She looked away, suddenly uncomfortable. Here she was, criticising and thinking snide thoughts. She remembered the ski jacket and the suede ankle boots, expensive items that must have cost more than the fostering allowance. No wonder Mrs Carmichael had looked hurt that morning.

Jamey was rigged out in a little green track-suit with three shorts and shirt sets to fill out his wardrobe. Shoes posed a bit of a problem because he had long feet with high arches.

'I think he should be a much bigger boy,' Mr Carmichael said as he carried Jamey through the precinct in his new jacket. 'We'll have to build him up . . . give him some muscles!'

On the words 'build' and 'muscles' Lisa could see that he was hugging and tickling Jamey until he squirmed and giggled. It was a lovely sound, that chuckle. It was a different 'Pop' from the one who had dragged Lisa off the pier. Lisa felt herself warming to him, just a little.

'I think Lisa could do with some new jeans,' Mrs Carmichael said as they passed a boutique.

'Please don't bother, I'm fine,' Lisa said. 'Get things

for Jamey.'

'Our "allowance" will run to jeans this month, Lisa,' Mrs Carmichael said, her head on one side and a faint smile playing round her mouth.

Lisa blushed. She had asked for that!'

It was a lovely Saturday. They even had tea out and Lisa could choose. Pizza was her favourite food and the local Deep Pan Pizza was the best. Jamey tucked in too and they all laughed at the thought of the little Billy Bunter he would be before long.

He fell asleep on her knee that night then clung to her as she put him into his bed.

'He didn't want to let go,' she said when she went downstairs.

'He loves you, because you've shown him love,' Mrs Carmichael said.

Lisa thought about that as she lay in bed. She was happier just then than she had been for a long time and Mrs Carmichael had been nice even though Lisa's comment about money had hurt her. Mr Carmichael had been nice too and she'd really been rude to him . . . more than once. It didn't make sense.

She went over the events of the day again and again and all the time Mrs Harris kept popping up in her thoughts.

'Why don't you talk to Jesus? He listens!'

Maybe Jesus had listened and had sent Jamey to help her to love again and feel wanted. Jamey's arrival had certainly made her look at her foster parents in a new light, a brighter one.

She knew something was wrong as soon as she got off the bus! The girl in front of her was wearing a bright blue anorak and the girl with her a lilac shell suit!

Lisa Fisher was noted for the flouting of school rules but most girls stuck to regulation grey. And here was a lilac dwarf, right in front of her!

It was earlier than usual, for Lisa, and she managed to get to her form room without meeting too many people.

She had made some resolutions – to try to be friendly and, most important, to behave in class – but the more people she saw the less she thought of her good intentions!

'It's a non-uniform day!' she gasped, within earshot of half the class.

'Of course it is, stupid! Why else are we dressed up!' It was Carrie . . . who else!

'We are, she isn't!' somebody sniggered and it spread around the room until everybody was having a good laugh, at her expense!

'When was this organised?' Lisa asked, not very politely.

'Last week!'

It was still Carrie . . . always Carrie who held the floor!

'I was in last week, most of it!' Lisa complained.

'You weren't in on Wednesday, not for long anyway!'

'Well somebody could have told me!' Lisa said, her voice rising in anger.

'Why? Are you supposed to be somebody special?' Carrie mocked, playing to her audience.

All the good feelings and the resolve to try left Lisa at that moment. The Carmichaels, Jamey and everything she had begun to value flew out of the classroom window.

'I'm a match for you any day, Carrie Rogers!'

'In what?'

'In anything you want!'

'Get lost, Lisa Fishface! You're all talk and no action. We've heard it all before!' Carrie shouted, backing away and not so sure of her ability to handle this situation.

Lisa's eyes were flashing and her face was red with

anger. Her fists were clenched and Carrie didn't like the look of that.

'Pack it in, Lisa . . . I don't want any trouble,' she said.

'No? Well I do! It's what you all expect isn't it? Lisa Fisher mouthing off . . . putting on a show . . . doing what you daren't do!' Lisa growled. 'So here's the best yet, Rogers. *You'll* be Fishfaced when I've done with you . . . BATTERED!'

'I'm going to get Mrs Foster. She's off her trolley, she is!' Carrie said, edging towards the door.

Lisa got there first though and stood with her back against it, fists ready.

'You're not going anywhere,' she said. 'You're all rotten pigs. You made sure I didn't know just to make me look stupid, the only stupid cow in uniform . . . Well, who looks stupid now?'

Carrie did! She was really scared and had begun to cry.

Lisa knew that they could be seen through the glass in the door and that it wouldn't be long before Foster came running to interfere, but she didn't care. Carrie Rogers was going to get it, once and for all!

'Stop it, Lisa,' Joy said, trying to get between Lisa and the two desks that kept her from Carrie. 'Mrs Foster's coming . . . you'll be in terrible trouble.'

'What's new?' Lisa snapped, still glaring at Carrie.

'She's coming!' Laura Evans gasped, spotting the tall figure of the Year Head charging down the corridor.

It was as though a signal had been given. Lisa launched herself across the desks, pushing Joy aside and knocking Carrie to the floor. Carrie tried to defend herself against Lisa's fury, pulling hair and scratching as she struggled to get away.

'Stop it right now!'

The voice had authority and the hands that wrenched

the girls apart were strong. It wasn't only Mrs Foster.
She had given the command but Mr Simpson was holding Lisa and he was six feet four! Even so, he found it
difficult to hold the kicking, writhing Lisa without hurting her.

'Whoa! Young lady. Steady on, you'll hurt yourself!'

'Not as much as I'll hurt her!' Lisa cried, in tears.

Carrie was holding a handkerchief to her mouth which
was bleeding from a gash on her lower lip. Lisa had a
scratch right down the left side of her face.

'My room!' Mrs Foster ordered and Lisa obeyed.

Suddenly all the fight had gone out of her and she
knew she had gone too far. There was only out outcome.
Fighting resulted in suspension . . . put out of school
and only re-admitted after an appeal to the governors,
by parents. Lisa couldn't see the Carmichaels standing
up for her after this.

Everything had gone wrong again! They sat in the
entrance hall, Lisa at one side, Carrie at the other. Each
stared straight ahead down the drive watching for the
car that would collect her, Carrie the sleek BMW and
Lisa the Red Flash.

As it turned out it was a harrassed Mrs Carmichael in
a taxi after searching for someone to have Jamey for an
hour.

'Oh Lisa,' she sighed. 'And I thought we were doing
so well!'

~ 6 ~

Mr Carmichael was livid.

He paced up and down the lounge with his hands clasped behind his back, shaking his head from side to side as if he had heard something unbelievable.

Jamey had started to scream as soon as the row started so Mrs Carmichael had taken him out of the way, even though it was his 'Eetha' he was crying for. The raised voices had really upset him.

Lisa's teeth were clenched together so tightly that she could feel each one pressing into her gums. She was aware that one at the back was hurting, with quick stabs of pain, but she couldn't tell which. Something inside her head was wittering on about making appointments to see the dentist and she kept thinking . . . I've got to look after my teeth. It was hilarious what the brain did all by itself!

'What does one have to do to sort you out, Lisa? All your life ahead of you! All the chances that Mom and me never had, I just can't reckon you up!'

There he went again, using that stupid American word for mother! Well, I'm not American and she's not my mother, she thought, glaring at the stiff-backed figure dancing about in front of her. All he needed was a bristling moustache to complete the picture.

'You don't have to. I don't want you to reckon me up . . . I just want you to leave me alone. Nobody ever understands!' Lisa screamed.

'Understands what? That you're incapable of staying out of trouble? You seem to thrive on it . . . even go looking for it!'

'It wasn't my fault!'

'Of course it was your fault. You attacked another girl and there were twenty others there watching, all ready to tell!' Mr Carmichael pointed out.

'You don't know what she . . . !'

Lisa was cut off in mid sentence. 'I'm not interested in what she did. It's what *you* did that counts. Whatever it was you imagine she did doesn't merit that kind of behaviour. Nothing does!'

Lisa folded her arms and sulked. What was the use? It was all going to be her fault, as usual.

'And I was thinking of calling you Pop!' she sneered.

'You needn't bother. You'll have to be a different girl before that would please me.'

'Thanks for nothing,' Lisa spat out as she got up and made for the door.

'I didn't give you permission to leave the room!'

She gave that sigh and the lift of her shoulders that had become her trade-mark.

'Please may I leave the room?' she lisped in a simpering 'little girl' voice.

She didn't wait for an answer but flung open the door and stamped up the stairs.

'You'd better stay there too!' Mr Carmichael called after her. 'We'll discuss this later, when we've all calmed down.'

'Not if I can help it. I'm out of here . . . for good!'

Lisa took off her school uniform, flinging it about the

room. Her skirt landed on the little bed and for a moment the thought of Jamey stopped her in the tracks. She did love him!

In spite of that love and in the certain belief that it would be taken away from her like everything else, she pulled on her jogging bottoms and a sweatshirt, replacing her posh ankle boots with her scruffy trainers. She was tying the laces when Mrs Carmichael opened the door. She was holding Jamey in her arms and he was crying bitterly. Lisa longed to take him and cuddle him.

'Will you come downstairs and talk about this, Lisa?'

'I'll come downstairs, but I'm not discussing anything!' Lisa replied, pushing past Mrs Carmichael and jumping down the stairs three at a time.

Before anyone could stop her she was out of the front door and running down the street like a hundred metre sprinter . . . fast! Each pounding footstep jarred her whole body but she kept on running, unaware of her surroundings and the people she passed as she left trouble behind.

Lisa Fisher, Lisa Fisher. Needn't bother, needn't bother.

The words rang in her head in time with her feet until she collapsed, exhausted, against a rickety old fence.

Once she had her breath back and could think about something else but her pounding heart, she studied her surroundings.

'Allotments!'

She said it aloud, surprised to find herself there. The allotments were right across town. Either she had run right through the centre, traffic and all, or she had run on the ring road . . . and that was miles! Either way she couldn't remember a thing!

Most of the little vegetable plots were well cultivated with greenhouses and potting sheds. In one an elderly couple were pottering about among tall bean poles and in another an old man was weeding between rows of green plants that could have been anything.

It was very peaceful. Lisa stuck her face under a rather rusty tap and drank a little of the cold water, splashing her feet and legs.

'You don't want to be drinking that, love,' an elderly lady called out from behind a hedge. 'I've got some dandelion and burdock in my shed if you want some.'

'Right!' Lisa said, wiping her face with the back of her hand. 'Thanks, I do!'

The shed was a little palace. 'I spend all my afternoons here,' the lady said as she poured Lisa a glass of the fizzy pop from a thermos flask. 'I grow all my own potatoes and greens. You should see my tomatoes!'

Lisa smiled. It was a well kept garden.

'It keeps me busy and ekes out the pension you know. You have to do what you can these days. Are you looking for somebody?'

Lisa took another drink before she answered. It gave her time to think.

'Er . . . Yes, my grandad . . . right over there,' she lied, waving her arm towards a spot as far away from the old girl as possible. To add credibility to her claim she said thank you for the drink and set off purposefully towards the far side of the allotments where some of the plots were untended and overgrown. Some had skeletal greenhouses and roofless sheds . . . obviously abandoned or left by somebody now deceased. They were sad places, unlike the old girl's patch.

'Unloved like me!' Lisa grunted, eyeing the derelict sheds.

One wasn't!

The door swung on one hinge, but it closed, and there was a latch to hold it in place. Inside, some old man had made a place to sit and contemplate his empire. There was an ancient deckchair, its striped ticking faded and green in places with mould. A large pine chest of drawers stood against the back wall and an unsteady card-table held two plates, a knife and an old newspaper. The smell of rotting wood and gentle decay revived old memories and Lisa lowered herself into the canvas chair. It held her weight and with a sigh she settled down to rest, and remember . . .

. . . 'Nana . . . Nana! Can I play in the shed please, can I, Nana? Can I?'

'Can I, Nana! That's all I ever hear. What are you after now?'

'Stop bothering Nana, Lisa,' her mother said, as she scraped new potatoes for lunch.

'She's not bothering me at all, Margaret. I like to hear her prattle . . . What do you want, love?'

'Can I make a house in the old shed?'

Lisa was visiting her grandmother, her mother's mother. Mrs Gregg lived in the middle of a row of tiny cottages that had once been built for farm workers. Now the farm had gone and the little village was on the edge of a large town, becoming part of Uttley as its need for housing spread its boundaries.

The cottage had low-beamed ceilings and a twisty staircase led up to the two bedrooms. Mrs Gregg had extended the back of the cottage to make a bathroom that looked out over the garden. It was impossible to see the countryside at the end of the garden because it was so long!

Although it was only as wide as the cottage, the garden seemed to go on for ever. First of all there was a flagged patio with chimney pots full of geraniums and an old stone sink overflowing with nasturtiums and fuchsia. Three stone steps rose in the middle of a holding wall and then there was a square lawn with a border all round. All sorts of plants made up the border and there was always a lovely show, all year. Lisa liked the tall holly-hocks that grew against the side walls.

Beyond the lawn and a fence made out of twisted tree branches, six fruit trees made a little orchard. Five of them were apple trees and one produced really juicy pears that Lisa loved to eat.

Behind the orchard was the vegetable plot that Grandpa Gregg had laid out before he died. Nana grew a few rows of garden peas and climbing beans but most of the plot was overgrown.

Right at the end of the narrow garden and against the wall that divided it from a grassy meadow was a hen coop. It had a run of bare earth enclosed in rusty wire netting in front of it.

It took all the rest of the holiday but Lisa swept out the hen coop, scrubbed the floor clean of ancient droppings, painted the inside with half a tin of white emulsion paint left over from the bedroom ceilings and furnished it with a wooden box for a table and a three-legged stool.

Nana let her use an old pegged rug that had been on the bedroom floor before the new carpet arrived and that, and a few chipped cups and odd saucers gave Lisa her very own house.

There were two little girls living in the street and they came to play, bringing their dolly prams and 'babies'. Sometimes the hen coop was a doctor's surgery and Lisa examined and weighed the babies, handing out medicine wrapped in bits of tissue – little pebbles and spoonfuls of dry dusty earth.

Sometimes it was a school with Lisa the teacher but most often it was Lisa's house where her friends came to visit and take tea with her.

It was her special place . . .

. . . 'My place!'

Lisa sat up and looked around her. The walls were

intact and the shed was dry. It had been a wet spring yet nothing had come through the roof! The window glass was dirty but unbroken and although two boards had rotted away in one corner the floor was solid everywhere else. She stamped about to check it.

It was an idea that formed quickly and once formed it filled Lisa's thoughts.

It wasn't easy to go back to the house and apologise. The Carmichaels were having a late tea when Lisa walked in. Mrs Carmichael looked relieved and Jamey stuck out his arms and squeaked 'Eetha', bouncing up and down in her arms when she picked him up for a hug.

Mr Carmichael studied his plate as though it held buried treasure.

Lisa put Jamey back in the high chair and cleared her throat.

'I'm sorry,' she said.

'Is that all?'

Mrs Carmichael gave her husband a look that said . . . careful!

'Would you like some tea?' she asked.

'Yes please,' Lisa said, sliding into her seat next to Jamey. She gave his hand a squeeze.

After tea, when Jamey was in bed, there was a conference. Lisa was allowed to give her side of the affair and, for once, wasn't interrupted.

Mrs Carmichael agreed that it was unkind of the class to keep the non-uniform day a secret from her but Mr Carmichael pointed out that she would have known all about it if she hadn't played truant.

'Young people today have no idea how valuable a good education is. They fritter it all away!'

Lisa stifled a yawn. It was so tedious!

'It's your whole attitude, Lisa. You just don't like authority. Everybody has to follow the rules, all through life. It doesn't end when you grow up either; we still have to conform to society's laws!' Mr Carmichael lectured.

Lisa tried not to show her lack of interest in society and its laws. She nodded and smiled to show that she understood and agreed with what he was saying even though she was thinking . . . What a prat!

He seemed to go on for ever and there were several moments when Lisa wanted to argue and shout but she didn't. Her plans needed time and there was a lot to organise. She didn't want to rock the boat until she was good and ready.

'So, we have an interview with the Headmistress and the Chairman of Governors in three days and then you should be allowed back in school next Monday as long as you agree to toe the line.'

One week! It wasn't long but it would have to do.

Lisa was up early on Tuesday morning.

'Is there anything you want me to do?' she asked.

Mrs Carmichael smiled. 'Not really, unless tidying your room is a good idea? I'm taking Jamey to the shops in a while. Would you like to come? We could have lunch in town.'

Lisa would have loved to go shopping in town and have lunch, but there were more important things on her mind.

'No thanks. I'll do my room, then go for a run. It's sports day soon and I need to put in some training in case I make the finals. The long distance heats are coming up in a couple of weeks,' Lisa said.

Mrs Carmichael beamed, pleased with her answer. When she smiled like that her cheeks stuck out like two table-tennis balls and her raised eyebrows lifted the whole of her hair, as though it was a wig.

Lisa had to turn away to stop herself laughing.

'Can you get your own lunch then? We'll make a day of it, won't we, Jamey . . . take you to see the donkeys, eh?' Mrs Carmichael said, ruffling Jamey's hair and wiping the egg-yolk from his chin with a corner of her pinafore.

'What time will you be back?' Lisa asked.

'On the three o'clock bus, if it doesn't rain.'

'I'll run after lunch then I won't have to take a key. You'll be back before me. I'll meet the bus and help you carry the shopping if you like,' Lisa offered.

She cleaned the bedroom until Mrs Carmichael left with Jamey then she gathered the things she needed. There was an old shopping bike in the garage, one with small wheels and a basket and it only took a minute to pump up the tyres. The name JENNIFER was scratched in the paint of the crossbar.

A scrubbing brush, a new packet of soap powder, a dishcloth and three old rags used for car cleaning; two blue checked tea towels and a packet of drawing pins, a small dustpan and brush and a bucket from the garage were stowed, hung and tied in the basket and on the handlebars and pillion of the bike.

Lisa made sure the house was locked and secure before she pedalled off towards the ring road. It stretched away into the distance and the traffic was quite heavy but there was a cycle path for most of the way. She was surprised how far she had run the day before. It was a long hard road even on a bike!

Once at the allotments she pushed the bike down a different path, approaching her plot from the other side. She didn't want to meet the old lady again.

The time flew by and although she only had cold water Lisa made quite an impression on the dirty shed. Once the windows were cleaned it was much lighter inside and the cobwebs were easy to see. She swept down the walls with a wet hand-brush and scrubbed the floor and the chest of drawers. It didn't look too bad. The tea cloths made reasonable looking curtains, pinned to the wooden window frames, and by the time she had to leave Lisa was pleased with 'her place'. It looked derelict from the path and the windows could only be seen by passengers on the trains that ran along the track behind the allotments. It was a safe haven.

'She really has taken what I said to heart,' Mr Carmichael said later that night. He was feeling pleased with himself. 'She's a different girl!'

'If only you knew!' Lisa muttered under her breath as she listened in to the conversation by the lounge door. 'If only you knew!'

By the weekend the shed was transformed. A well scrubbed drawer, raised on a pile of bricks gleaned from the surrounding plots, made an adequate cot for a little boy. Lisa had taken three blankets out of a storage chest in the little bedroom. They weren't used now that all the beds had duvets. A 20p cushion from the local charity shop completed the bedding and a crocheted poncho, made of brightly coloured wool in daisy shapes, covered the worn canvas on the deckchair.

Lisa had found two lengths of wood in a rubbish skip and they rested on two sets of iron brackets that must have held shelving at one time. They were stout and secure.

A pot of white paint taken from the garage had worked wonders and all the place needed was a rug of some sort, but that could wait. Lisa took quite a lot from the Carmichael home, things that wouldn't be missed immediately. A vase, a stainless steel tray she found at the back of the sideboard cupboard, two knives, a fork and a spoon, two odd plates, a mug and bowl she said she had broken while washing up, and three emergency candles she found in a box under the stairs.

The rest she stole.

Kev had shown her how easy it was and Lisa proved to be a clever thief.

She stocked the top drawer of the chest with biscuits,

crisps, cartons of long-life milk, fizzy orange and Cola in cans and a supply of chocolate and sweets that would last for ages. She took things she didn't need too. It became a sort of challenge – to see what she could get away with.

Teddy bears of all shapes and sizes and an assortment of other furry creatures sat on one of the shelves alongside toy cars, a little wooden train, picture books and jigsaw puzzles while the top of the chest of drawers held an array of pottery figurines, fancy dishes, bottles of perfume and other toiletries.

Stealing was easy.

The vase she filled with flowers cut from one of the plots devoted to blooms. They looked nice on the card table draped in an old net curtain. Once or twice Lisa thought she heard her Nana's voice . . . 'It does look nice, Lisa!' . . . and she nodded in agreement.

'Nearly ready, Nana, nearly done,' she whispered.

The Friday interview was a success. Lisa played the part of a suitably contrite miscreant and was forgiven, to start Monday on a mutually agreed behaviour pattern bound by a contract. It was all so stupid. Did they really think that signing a piece of paper would guarantee her good behaviour?

On Saturday Lisa went to town by herself, supposedly to buy a new file and A4 pad . . . to make a new start! Mr Carmichael gave her a five pound note to get what she needed and she said thank you very prettily. He was pleased by her attitude and even waved as she left.

'Silly old fool!' she muttered, then felt a pang of guilt. He was trying to be nice . . . 'But it won't last!' she said aloud, 'It never does – not for Lisa Fisher!'

Pushing her guilty feelings away Lisa made for the pier.

'Haven't seen you for ages. Been grounded?' Kev

asked, slipping his arm around her waist as though he had the right. Lisa wanted to push him away but she didn't, he was too useful.

'I'm having a bit of trouble, at home,' she said, leaning against him and smiling. 'I need some help.'

'What sort of help? Want me to duff up your old man? I've got contacts who'll put the boot in. Just say the word.'

'No, nothing like that,' Lisa said, biting her lip and lowering her eyes.

'Here! You're not . . . having a . . . ?'

'No, I'm not!' Lisa snapped. 'It's money. I need a lot quickly. I've been taking it from a tin box and if they find out I'll get sent back to a home. I've got to put it back.'

Lisa was putting a sob in her voice and she could see that Kev believed every word.

'How much?'

'Ten pounds . . . nearly.'

Kev laughed. 'I thought you meant hundreds the way you're carrying on! A tenner's nothing!'

'Will you lend it me then?' Lisa asked, all wide-eyed and trusting.

'Haven't got it chick . . . but, where there's a Kev there's a solution!'

Lisa won well over ten pounds on the machines with Kev's help and then said she had to leave.

'Hang on a minute, doll. One good turn and all that. What's in it for me?'

Kev had hold of her arm and his grip was hard and suddenly unfriendly.

'I've just put my job on the line so I'm entitled to something!'

He was steering her through the arcade to the shadows on the open part of the pier and for the first time Lisa felt scared.

'I don't want to go out there!' she said, struggling and freeing her arm. 'And definitely not with you!'

She kicked out with one booted foot, feeling it jar against his shin, then legged it through the arcade, along the prom and lost herself in the maze of streets behind, thankful for her training and her stamina for running. She called at a store and bought the file, her cover, and arrived home tired but with money in her pocket, money she needed in case she had to move out of the area. She was very pleasant and helpful all evening.

'Isn't it nice to share a family evening?' Mr Carmichael said, beaming at Lisa with Jamey on his knee.

On Sunday morning Mr and Mrs Carmichael announced that they would like to go to church and asked Lisa to look after Jamey.

It was exactly what she wanted.

Once they had left, Lisa dressed Jamey in his warm tracksuit and packed his pushchair with as much as she could of his clothes and toys. Her own stuff – clean underclothes and an extra jogging suit – she stuffed in her duffle bag to sling over her shoulder. From the kitchen she took a sliced loaf, the butter from the fridge, a pot of jam, two oranges and the boiled ham Mrs Carmichael had bought for Sunday tea.

Then, without looking back, she pushed Jamey towards the ring road and the long walk to the allotments.

It was a sunny day and Jamey enjoyed the walk, falling asleep about half way. When he woke up he was already in his 'drawer' and Lisa was making jam sandwiches.

'Dinner time, Jamey. Just you and me, together,' she said, lifting Jamey out of the drawer and onto her knee. 'Just you and me, where nobody can find us . . .'cos nobody wants us and we don't want them, do we?'

They had a great afternoon. Jamey played with the new toys Lisa had stolen for him and looked at the picture books until it got too dark. They had boiled ham sandwiches, crisps and an orange for supper then Jamey was undressed and put to bed in the drawer. He didn't like it at all and whimpered for ages until he fell into an uneasy sleep.

Lisa lit one candle when she was sure the plots would be empty and no-one would see the light round the ill-fitting door. It started to rain and that made a terrible noise on the corrugated tin roof, waking Jamey again but this time he screamed his loudest.

Somewhere a dog barked and a late train roared past, making them both jump. Jamey cried even louder and Lisa joined him.

It was dark, cold and scary alone in the empty allot-ments. There were strange noises and a scratching that could be mice, or rats. Something pattered over the roof and the candle sputtered as a cold draught filtered through the cracks around the door.

Lisa had her back to the window. The tea towels wouldn't close and she was frightened to turn round in case someone was looking in. She wished she had hung her jacket over the gap between the towels.

With Jamey cuddled on her knee under the two blankets Lisa spent an awful night in the deckchair. It was cold, dark and very lonely.

It wasn't a bit like Nana's hen coop.

~ 7 ~

'What time did you realise something was wrong, Mr Carmichael?' PC Watts asked, scribbling something in a little black book all the time he was talking.

Mr Carmichael looked at his wife and raised his eyebrows.

'Well, we came back from church and they weren't in then, but I thought Lisa had taken Jamey for a walk. That's reasonable, isn't it?' Mrs Carmichael said, her face white and her fingers pulling at the edge of the tablecloth.

The policeman wrote in his book then looked at his watch.

'It's six-thirty and you called us at six . . .'

'What are you saying?' Mr Carmichael said, getting up and leaning on the table. 'That we didn't ring soon enough?'

'We thought Lisa had taken him for a walk and lost count of time, or called at a friend's and got talking. We didn't think to look in drawers and wardrobes . . . why should we?' Mrs Carmichael sobbed. 'Who would imagine she'd run off with him?'

'And why aren't you out looking?' Mr Carmichael cried, banging his hand on the table. 'We waited, to give her the benefit of the doubt. When it got to tea-time we did look upstairs and then we called. She's taken Jamey, clothes and food . . . and one or two odds and ends as far as we can tell. No money mind, she's not taken a penny and there's plenty around.' Mr Carmichael sat down again, his usually straight back bent with worry.

'Could you make a list of what's gone, what she's taken? Anything that might be traced?' the policeman asked.

'Could *you*? Could you tell what bits and pieces had gone from your house? We don't keep a detailed list. You only know something's gone when you want it and can't find it!' Mr Carmichael complained, dropping into his chair and banging his elbow on the table. 'How many odd spoons do you have? How about dusters, or rags . . . lost any lately?' he went on, rubbing his elbow angrily.

Mrs Carmichael tried to keep calm and when a policewoman arrived she confided that there had been trouble with Lisa, over a period of time.

'We just want them found, both of them,' she said, closing her hand over her husband's as it lay on the table.

PC Watts put his notebook away, his eyes on the two hands that gripped each other with worry.

'Right then, we'll be off. There's a call out and there'll be a search,' he said.

'We would like you both to stay here, in case Lisa comes back tonight . . . and ring us if she . . .'

'We'll be right here,' Mrs Carmichael nodded.

They were still at the table when Miss Taylor called.

'Lisa feels unwanted and worthless, that's obvious,' she said. 'Particularly after what she suffered at her father's . . .'

'What? What are you talking about?' Mr Carmichael said, getting to his feet.

He was very angry when he heard of the interview

with Miss Taylor.

'Did nobody think it reasonable to inform my wife and me about it?' he yelled, banging his hand down on the table for the second time that night. 'We're trying to help the girl . . . or hadn't you noticed?'

'It was a confidential meeting, Mr Carmichael. We can't break a trust, it's policy!'

'Policy or not, it's just not on. How can we deal with problems we don't know about? She's a difficult girl, we know that . . . and we don't seem to have been much help, do we?'

Mrs Harris called too, at about eight o'clock.

'She's a troubled girl, isn't she?' she said, and the Carmichaels had to agree.

'We've tried, but not hard enough by the look of it.' Mrs Carmichael was near to tears as she spoke and walked to the window. 'It's getting dark,' she said. 'Where is she?'

'And where's Jamey?' Mr Carmichael added.

'Safe, I'm sure,' his wife said quietly, crossing to the table and squeezing his shoulder. 'Lisa loves him.'

Lisa did love Jamey. She kept telling herself that as she tried to stop him crying. It was light outside and she could hear voices. People were unlocking sheds and exchanging pleasantries. It seemed that Jamey had been shrieking for hours and she had fed him crisps, Coke and chocolate but nothing had worked.

'They'll hear you Jamey . . . Hush . . . Hush now . . . Please be quiet Jamey . . . Jamey . . . JAMEY!'

He was quiet, for a stunned moment after Lisa's hand slapped hard against his face. Then, as his cheek reddened, his mouth opened again.

She was horrified. She had done exactly as her father had done, lashed out in anger without caring that she hurt the little boy . . . as she had been hurt.

'I'm sorry, Jamey. I didn't mean it,' she wailed, cuddling him close and rubbing his cheek.

She was really crying, her face as wet as Jamey's as it rested against her cheek. He clung to her, his arms clasped tightly round her neck. Still holding him she moved to the door and opened it just a little, hoping the sight of gardens and sunshine would shut him up, but she shut it quickly as she saw the old 'fizzy pop' lady pointing at the hut. There was a crowd with her and in the middle of it Lisa could see the checked headband of a policewoman's hat.

'They must have heard you, Jamey. They've called the police, but they won't get us . . . the pigs!'

Without thinking she clutched Jamey in one arm as she flung open the door with the other and darted down the side of the hut towards the railway line. By the time her sudden dash had registered with the crowd she was scrambling over the wire and boarding and was half way up the embankment before the police gave chase.

Lisa found an almost superhuman strength as she ran, hardly feeling the burden in her arms as she crossed the line and went full tilt, down the opposite bank. She thought of nothing but escape and outran her pursuers as she made for the canal and the town beyond. Jamey had stopped struggling and was silent and Lisa only became aware of him as he squeezed her throat with his terrified arms.

At last, with her lungs bursting and her arms like lead she came to a bend in the canal where it went under the road and half fell down the brambled bank and into the darkness of the tunnel. It was quiet under the stone arches and the water looked like ink, the black ink in plastic bottles that was used in art, for drawing.

Apart from the rasp of her own breath, Lisa was aware of other noises . . . shouts in the distance and the rumble of cars as they passed over the canal hidden deep in its tunnel.

She stepped to the edge.

The canal had stone walls here, big square blocks of grey stone that disappeared into the inky water and looked green in places. She leaned over to see if she was reflected in the water . . . she wasn't. Even the canal didn't want to know her.

Her body shuddered with a great sigh that ended in a little whimper. Jamey was stiff in her arms and suddenly heavy. He was too frightened to move and his eyes were wide and staring.

It was as if time had stopped, ended.

There was an uncomfortable silence that made her look, with care, to right and left. In the circle of daylight at either end of the tunnel were uniformed figures, moving and pointing.

Lisa took a deep breath and stood up straight, letting Jamey slide down her body to the ground and holding on to him by the hood of his tracksuit. She saw an officer hold up his hand and the figures stopped moving.

For a moment she felt like laughing. What did they think she was going to do? Jump in?

Looking down into the dark water it didn't seem such a bad idea. Nobody would miss her. Nobody would weep for Lisa Fisher . . . Codface Fisher . . . Fishface!

She took another step forward until her toes were hooked over the edge, Jamey held tightly against her leg.

Think Lisa, Mrs Harris whispered inside her head. *Everything has a solution . . . There's a light at the end of every tunnel.*

Lisa looked at the light. There were policemen in it.

'No, there isn't!' she cried out.

'What's that, love . . . did you say something?'

The harsh male voice made Lisa jump. Mrs Harris was talking to her. Why did Mrs Harris sound like a man?

She didn't understand.

'I don't understand,' she whined in a very small voice.

'What? What don't you understand? Come on, love . . . come out where we can hear you, where we can help.'

'Where's Mrs Harris? I want . . .'

She stumbled, almost overbalancing and Jamey swung on the end of his hood until he was almost over the edge. He began to scream.

Talk to Jesus, he'll help, Mrs Harris whispered.

She couldn't see Mrs Harris. She could see a red cloud that screamed and there were patches of light.

'I can't see you!' she cried.

'Can't see who, love? Who do you want to see?' PC Watts called out, making her jump again.

Lisa was confused. Mrs Harris wanted her to talk to someone but she knew he wouldn't listen. Mrs Harris wasn't there, nobody was. She was all alone in a red cloud that screamed in her head.

Lisa Fisher is nobody, useless, worth nothing!

Lisa could hear the voice telling her she was worthless, but it wasn't until the red cloud dimmed and it was dark again that she realised it was her own voice.

She began to cry, great body-heaving sobs that took her breath away like hands around her throat, squeezing and pressing until her head spun and her stomach churned. She saw her father's angry face and almost felt his blows as he rejected her . . . she saw her mother leaving her as the coffin sank into the earth and she almost fell as she screamed.

Suddenly, all was confusion. There was a lot of shouting and Jamey wailed as he was swept up in a pair of strong arms as another policeman grabbed Lisa from behind. He held her tightly with her arms held to her sides as, with one swift movement, he lifted and moved her from the water's edge.

The sudden actions woke Lisa from her dream state with startling results.

She kicked out backwards making contact with the policeman's shins and butted his chest with the back of her head.

'Let me go, you rotten pig!' she yelled as she struggled to get free.

'Now calm down, young lady, we're only trying to help. It's for your own good!'

'How do you know what's good for me? You don't know me! Nobody does . . . and nobody wants to!'

Several more uniformed figures, silhouetted against the circles of light, were hurrying towards the struggling pair.

'Hold her!' someone cried.

Lisa fought as hard as she could. She refused to walk and was half carried, kicking and screaming, to a waiting police car. They weren't rough with her at all, just held her close until the car moved off.

'Where are you taking me? Where's Jamey?' Lisa gasped. 'I want Jamey, I don't want to go with you!'

'That's enough now, love . . . everything's all right . . . everybody's safe now.'

Lisa felt all the anger drain away. What was the point? They always won, didn't they? Always got their way? Everybody won but Fishface . . . she didn't deserve to.

'You just don't understand do you?' she whispered to no-one in particular.

She was so tired . . . so very, very tired.

It was morning. A single shaft of sunlight streamed through a half inch gap in the curtains and was reflected in the square of mirror over the sink.

Lisa stared at the sink, then at the narrow wardrobe and the three drawer chest.

It was not her room. There was no fitted carpet in

her favourite shade of blue, no lampshade to match the curtains and no music centre and shelf of tapes.

It was not her room.

She closed her eyes and opened them again, twice, hoping that it was all a bad dream. It wasn't!

She knew when she was summoned to breakfast that this was not another children's home. Her door was not locked but at the end of the short corridor outside her room was a circular space with more corridors leading from it, like a hub in the centre of a wheel.

At the hub was a small office with glass walls and inside she could see a uniformed woman watching several TV sets . . . watching the corridors.

It was not a community home!

Lisa was trembling so much she could hardly walk. The woman who had come for her was holding her by the elbow, very gently, and walked at her pace up the corridor and down another. The officer in the glass room turned to look at her and smiled. She couldn't make her mouth smile back.

Where was she?

Lisa couldn't remember anything except the canal and the inky water. What had happened? Where was Jamey?

She felt sick and found it hard to breathe and her own heartbeat pounded in her ears.

'Come along, Lisa, let's get some breakfast into you, then you'll feel much better.'

The room was small and square and there were two tables and several plastic chairs. Through the one window Lisa could see a brick wall and a bush with pale purple flowers. There was nothing to show where she was.

It was very clean. At one table a dark-haired girl about Lisa's age was spooning porridge into her mouth. A woman sat by her at the table and another, in uniform, stood by a serving hatch that revealed a small kitchen.

The girl didn't look up as Lisa sat at the other table to attempt to eat her breakfast . . . lukewarm and lumpy porridge and a poached egg on two slices of toast. The cutlery was plastic, as was the mug of tea.

All the time she was eating, her corridor companion stood watching, then another uniformed figure entered and stood by the door.

Lisa couldn't imagine why four people were there to watch two girls eat breakfast.

She finished her meal in silence, forcing it down with great gulps of tea. Running away would take strength and stamina and Lisa was already planning to do just that!

'Get up, Debbie!' The strident voice made Lisa jump. Debbie didn't move.

'Get up, Debbie, please!'

Debbie did. She sprang to her feet, pushed over the table and picked up the chair but before she could do anything with it two strong pairs of arms had grabbed her and hustled her, kicking and screaming abuse, out of the room.

Lisa began to shake and the red clouds gathered again as her own high pitched whine filled her ears and the hot tears fell.

The small office was furnished with comfortable chairs and a tiled coffee table. There were paintings on the walls, and photographs of lovely places.

The woman who had fetched her to breakfast was there, standing by the door, watching. Another sat, relaxed and smiling, in one of the soft chairs.

'Sit down, Lisa, I'm Miss Elliot.'

It was an Assessment Centre, and Lisa was there to be 'assessed'. She was there to determine why she was violent, how violent she was and how she could best be helped. It was a centre for finding out all about Lisa

Fisher and why she felt worthless and unwanted. It was also designed to determine what was best for her . . . what to do with her . . . how to help her socially, educationally and emotionally. It was all explained at great length.

'You're for the nut house Leez!' Debbie jibed. 'You ought to scream and kick their heads in . . . that gets 'em going, then they leave you alone for a bit.'

Debbie caused as much trouble as she could.

Lisa did, and said, nothing. She hadn't said anything since the first day. She listened passively to Debbie's tales of running away . . . abuse from her father and brother . . . excursions to large shopping centres to steal things to sell . . . wild parties with drink and pills and what she'd done with her many boyfriends, but made no comment.

Debbie didn't care about anyone or anything. 'I'm just waiting to be sixteen, then I can do what I like. You won't see me for dust . . . and next time I'll finish it!'

Debbie had hit her brother with a brick.

Miss Elliot tried hard to get through to Lisa but she retreated into a private world. She ate, slept and did as she was told . . . and that was all.

~ 8 ~

Lisa was walking through waist high sponge, forcing herself forward while two large suitcases, attached to a chain around her neck, bumped along behind.

There were people floating on pink candyfloss, calling to her as she struggled.

'Empty the suitcases, Fishface! What have you got in there?'

'Things!' Lisa gasped. 'My things.'

'Get rid of them,' an old man said, wagging a finger. 'Things aren't good for you!'

'All things?' Lisa asked.

'Those things that drag you down!'

The dream changed. She was riding the waves of a black river in an empty suitcase. There were people on the bank and they were trying to throw things into the suitcase. One or two landed but it still floated, though it sank into the cold water until it lapped over the edges and her bare feet were wet and cold.

'Please . . . don't throw any more in, I'll sink,' she begged.

Suddenly it went dark and there was a burst of shrill laughter as something big and heavy fell into the 'boat'.

'There's your biggest burden, Fishface . . . Guilty! Guilty! Guilty!' The boat sank and the water was cold, so cold as it closed over her head.

The flowered duvet was on the floor when the buzzer went.

Lisa was cold. She looked at her watch. It was seven-thirty.

After the first week, when it was obvious that Lisa wasn't likely to hurt herself or damage her surroundings, she had been given a much nicer room. The furniture matched and the curtains were pretty. She had her music centre thoughtfully sent by the Carmichaels, though they hadn't been allowed to visit her. All the tests had to be completed first.

The room was never locked and there was a shower room next to it. Lisa let the hot jets warm life back into her stiff limbs, then hurried into her skirt and jumper to wait for breakfast.

'Are we going to say good morning, Lisa?' Joyce asked as she arrived to take her to the little dining room.

There was no answer. Lisa clenched her teeth, because anything she said was worthless and meaningless, so it was better to be silent, totally!

One of the rooms on C block was a classroom. There were three desks and nine chairs. Lisa sat at her desk with Joyce on her right. Joyce had never been far from her side since that first morning.

The teacher stood at the front by a white wall board. At the side of the board was a red button. A uniformed officer sat by the door.

There were three girls in class that morning, Lisa, Debbie and a very fat girl with spiky hair.

Lisa held her pen very loosely as the teacher began putting maths problems on the board. She gave a long explanation that made little sense to Lisa then told the girls to work out the answer on graph paper.

Lisa made no attempt to write. She never did. She knew that anything she wrote would be rubbish, so what was the point?

Debbie made an aeroplane out of her paper and threw it at the new girl.

There was a moment of stillness, as though someone had pressed the pause button on a video and stopped the action at one frame. Debbie sat with her arm in the air after releasing the paper dart and the new girl sat with the aeroplane impaled on her lacquered spikes. The three 'guardians' had faces frozen in surprise and the officer was half out of her chair reaching for the panic button.

The peace didn't last long!

The new girl let out a roar of anger and launched herself at Debbie, grabbing handfuls of hair as they both crashed to the floor. Their three 'guardians' sprang to their feet and made for the door. The officer slammed his hand on the button and set off the siren that brought two more into the room. All was confusion.

Lisa sat in her desk and watched, motionless, as the officers separated the fighting girls and carried them out by their arms and legs . . . limbs that were twisting and kicking with frustration and rage. Both girls were screaming abuse at each other and their captors as they were moved down the corridor and out of sight.

After the door closed Lisa was left alone with the teacher and Joyce. The teacher blew air out through her pursed lips.

'Well!' she said. 'What a performance that was! Aren't you glad you kept out of that commotion, Lisa?'

Both adults turned, not really expecting her to speak but anticipating a nod of agreement . . . or at the least, a smile. They got neither.

Lisa's head was flung back as though in spasms. Her glassy eyes were fixed on a point on the ceiling and tears were running down her pale cheeks. She was whimpering, making little high pitched noises and she was holding her breath. By the time Joyce reached her, she was shaking uncontrollably and her fists were clenched.

'No lessons today, I think!' the teacher said to Joyce.

Lisa was sick when she got back to her room. Being sick was interesting and gave her whole days in her room, in bed, where she could do absolutely nothing and see nobody. She was sick often.

Lisa withdrew, away from people, things, everything.

Mrs Harris sank wearily into her chair in the staffroom. 'An afternoon with 10C just about finishes me off,' she sighed. 'They really are a handful.'

'Not as bad as 10B when Lisa Fisher was holding forth. What a relief to be rid of her!' someone said.

Mrs Harris almost made an angry retort but thought better of it.

'A relief, yes,' she agreed. 'But did any of us try to find out why she was so . . .'

'Obnoxious?' Miss Dodds said. 'I'd rather not think about her, if you don't mind. Lessons have taken on a "honeymoon" feeling, pure paradise! She made my life hell!'

'She was a nice kid when I taught her lower down the school,' Mr Downes butted in. 'Something must have put her off.'

'I don't want to think about her . . . if you don't mind!' Miss Dodds said, closing her bag with a snap and ending the conversation.

Mrs Harris did think about Lisa though, quite a lot.

Carrie Rogers stayed behind after the RE lesson, at Mrs Harris's request. She was nervous and twisted the handle of her school bag into a knot she couldn't undo. She didn't think she had done anything wrong and was anxious to get to the sports hall and the badminton nets.

'Lisa's in real trouble, Carrie,' Mrs Harris said. 'And very unhappy. I'm going to go and see her. Would you like to send her a message, or anything?'

Carrie shrugged her shoulders. Her blonde ponytail swung from side to side as she bent to put her bag on a chair.

'We're not friends. She wouldn't welcome anything from me!' she muttered.

'You used to be! I can remember the "Terrible Two" who did everything together. You were like Siamese twins.'

'Well, things went a bit wrong when . . .'

Mrs Harris knew what Carrie was going to say. Things went wrong when Lisa's mother died.

'Tell me about it,' Mrs Harris said quietly.

Carrie thought for a minute.

'Lisa's mother died and it was awful,' she said. 'I didn't know about it at first because Lisa was taken away somewhere, to her father I think. I couldn't write to her because I didn't know where she was. Honestly, I didn't know what had happened to her!'

Mrs Harris could see that Carrie was getting upset so she pulled two chairs together for them to sit on.

'Go on, Carrie, what happened?'

'It wasn't my fault! I'd never known anybody who'd died. I liked Lisa's mum, she was really nice. I didn't know what to say! How can you tell somebody you're sorry . . . it doesn't mean anything!'

'So you avoided her?'

Carrie nodded. 'I kept out of her way so I wouldn't have to talk about it. I didn't want to talk about her mother dying. I didn't know how to . . . speak to her, it was embarrassing somehow. Then she started picking on me and calling me names! I hadn't done anything!'

Mrs Harris shook her head. 'We don't communicate very well, we humans. Many people are embarrassed by death, Carrie. Coping with another's sorrow isn't easy and usually people leave their bereaved friends alone in their grief . . . thinking it's for the best.'

'She didn't seem sorry at all! She was really nasty to everybody when she came back. I just didn't like her any more.' Carrie said, getting to her feet and throwing her bag over her shoulder. 'I just didn't know what to say! I couldn't say "I know how you feel" because I didn't. I've never had anybody die, who was close to me.'

She paused, then looked straight at Mrs Harris.

'Can you understand that?' she asked.

Mrs Harris smiled. 'Of course I can. And I know how bad feeling develops when people don't talk to each other. Lisa's going to need a friend, Carrie.'

'There's a lot of talk going around, about where Lisa is. Joy knows a boy who saw her being taken away in a police car,' Carrie said. 'Is it true she's gone to a Detention Centre?'

'Let's just say she's being helped, Carrie.'

'We were best friends,' Carrie said. 'I suppose it could be sorted out.'

Mrs Harris put an arm around her shoulder.

'I think you might have to make the first move, Carrie,' she said softly, as they left the classroom together.

Mrs Carmichael had Jamey under one arm and a pair of dungarees under the other when she opened the door to Mrs Harris.

'Do come in,' she said. 'This is a surprise.'

Mrs Harris accepted the offer of coffee then cleared her throat.

'I've been thinking about Lisa,' she began.

Mrs Carmichael sighed. 'She's still being assessed,' she explained. 'We've been asked to keep away for the time being. We did go, once, but she went wild and ran from us. It was awful, as though she hated us.'

'I'm sure she didn't . . . doesn't!' Mrs Harris said. 'She's just a bit mixed up. I wonder if she'd see me?'

'The psychiatrist seems to think it's depression, serious depression. She'll have to have treatment. We do want to see her and we do want her home!'

'In spite of everything?'

'Because of everything. She needs us, and Jamey.'

Mrs Harris was stunned when she saw Lisa.

She was sitting in the visitors' room almost dwarfed by the low armchair. She was thin, pale and her head was bowed, her chin almost on her chest.

'She doesn't say much these days,' Joyce said, plumping up the cushion behind her charge. 'Not to me, anyway. She doesn't react to much either. Can I leave her with you? She might open up if she's alone with you.'

'Is she allowed outside?' Mrs Harris asked, eyeing the double doors that led into a small walled garden.

'She'll go with you if you ask her. She always does as she's told.'

Once Joyce had left the room Mrs Harris pulled up a chair, sitting right in front of Lisa and so close that their knees touched. She leaned forward and took one of the hands held, so loosely, in Lisa's lap.

'Hello, Lisa,' she said. 'How are you, love?'

Lisa lifted her head very slowly and stared at her teacher. Her eyes were dull and it seemed that she was looking right through Mrs Harris, not at her.

'Lisa, I've come to see you. How are you feeling?'

There was a slight movement of the limp hand held in hers and Mrs Harris had to bite her lip to keep her own emotions in check.

'Whatever happened, Lisa? What have we done to you between us?'

Lisa moved her head ever so slightly and a tear trickled down the side of her nose.

'Come on, love, let's go and get a bit of sunshine.'

The two walked round and round the little paved square with its patch of grass and low shrubs. Lisa was silent but Mrs Harris talked for half an hour.

She discussed plants, colours and scents . . . Lisa's dress and hair and related all the gossip . . . Miss Dodds' new hair style, Mrs Foster's son joining the Air Force, the year 11 summer concert with the newly formed pop group . . . anything and everything until she ran out of breath.

Joyce called them back inside when it was Lisa's tea-time and the end of visiting.

'May I come again, Lisa?' Mrs Harris asked.

Lisa smiled. It was fleeting and the adults had to be on their toes to spot it but it was a smile.

'There! That's quite an improvement,' Joyce said. 'You must come again Mrs Harris!'

'She's very depressed,' the doctor told Mr and Mrs Carmichael. 'It's as though she has blanked out all the unpleasantness in her life . . . we have to dig it out again and help her to face her problems and come to terms with her life. We have done some tests and it is as we expected. Lisa places little or no value on herself. She really believes that she has nothing to offer. Her violent outbreaks got her noticed and that gave her a brief "lift". To a child who feels abandoned and rejected a good hiding is better than nothing, better than being ignored. It's a kind of attention-seeking that cries out for help.'

'And we didn't hear her, did we?' Mr Carmichael said sadly, shaking his head.

'You mustn't blame yourselves. It was just the last straw at the end of a whole stableful of straws.'

'She's so . . . withdrawn. I don't like to see her like

this!' Mrs Carmichael was almost in tears as they got up to leave. 'I want her home. I'd rather have her as she was than like this!'

Lisa was at the centre five weeks before she began to respond to people again.

Mrs Harris visited her twice a week, just talking to her about everyday things like shopping and supermarkets and the lovely sweater she had seen in a boutique in town. She talked about the girls at school too, watching closely when she mentioned Carrie. Gradually, a little at a time, Lisa opened out and began to take notice. Her eyes came alive again and once or twice Mrs Harris thought she detected just the slightest twinkle as she retold a story she'd heard about one of the juniors.

At the beginning of week six Lisa met Mr Adams who came in the afternoons.

Mr Adams was an artist who worked with the occupational therapists. He was full of ideas and enthusiasm and brought along all kinds of materials for painting and modelling.

Lisa was persuaded to try her hand at painting. She really liked the quick drying acrylic paint that she could use thickly, like oils, and spent her afternoons producing some very good pieces.

'You have real talent, Lisa,' Mr Adams said, his head on one side as he examined one painting. 'I like this one, everybody's smiling!'

Lisa's figures were simple and dressed in bright clothing . . . red trousers, yellow T-shirts and bright blue dungarees. All the figures had lots of curly hair and each one had a wide smile.

'Have you ever seen Lowry's work?' Mr Adams asked. 'Your paintings remind me of his . . . but most of his people are grey and black, hurrying to and from work in the mills and mines. Yours are all playing happily in the sunlight.'

Mrs Harris noticed it too. All Lisa's people were in groups, mum and dad and the children laughing in the sun. They all touched too, connected together by held hands, a hand on a shoulder or an arm around the waist.

Lisa smiled, gulped . . . and spoke. 'It would be nice to be like that, together,' she mumbled.

It was the beginning of the recovery. Lisa painted and talked, a little more each day and the improvement was obvious.

She was allowed an outing with Mrs Harris one Saturday afternoon. They looked in all the shops then went to the Art Gallery to see some paintings by L.S. Lowry.

Lisa liked them a lot. They weren't all dark. One that Lisa liked most was of a market and the people were all busy and happy. It made her feel good and Mrs Harris bought her a postcard of it from the Gallery gift shop.

To Lisa's surprise Mrs Harris stopped at a hairdressers called Waves.

'Come along,' she said. 'Let's see what they can do about your hair.'

Lisa's hair had grown quite a bit and hung in limp strands to her shoulders. The stylist looked at her from all angles.

'Can I have a free hand?' she asked.

Lisa nodded. She looked horrid anyway so anything she did would be an improvement.

The scissors clicked, the dryer hummed and Lisa's locks fell around her feet. The stylist cut her hair very short, like a boy's at the back but full on top and swept back.

'It's called a wedge,' the stylist explained. 'It's the latest!' It did look rather good!

'I like it,' Mrs Harris said as they left the shop and went to the car park. 'It suits you. You look really nice.'

Lisa felt the tears welling up inside her but managed to wait until they were in the car before letting them fall.

'I don't understand why you're so nice to me,' she cried. 'I'm not nice and I've been horrible to everybody. When I think of all the awful things I've said and done and all the trouble I've caused I'm so ashamed. I would understand if nobody bothered with me, ever again.'

Mrs Harris took her hand.

'You lost yourself for a while, Lisa, that's all. There are some things that knock the strongest of us sideways . . . onto the wrong path. But none of us are ever really lost. Once, when Jesus was talking to his disciples he told them to look after his children. By children he meant all of us, each one of his flock. When the shepherd loses one sheep he leaves the other ninety-nine in order to search for the lost one, and when he finds it he's overjoyed. At that moment that "lost but found" sheep means more to him than all those who didn't get lost.'

'And I'm a lost sheep?' Lisa asked, with a little smile.

'Found, Lisa. Lost but found.'

~ 9 ~

Joyce stood with the car door open.

'Come on, then!' she said. 'It's your first weekend at home so let's get going.'

Lisa gulped, feeling sick suddenly, and almost asked to go back to her room.

It had been a good day on the whole. Breakfast had been quiet and uneventful and the school day had gone well too. The teacher, with infinite patience had explained the work so slowly and carefully, and in three different ways until Lisa had understood. It was a new feeling . . . success . . . and the teacher had patted her on the back and praised her.

Then Miss Elliot said she could go home for the weekend, to see how things went.

Now she felt terrible and didn't want to go. What if it all went wrong?

It felt strange, outside, after so long in the centre. The sun was shining and she knew she should be feeling happy but there was a fluttering deep inside that made her feel sick, a feeling that got worse the nearer they got to the Carmichaels' house.

'I'm going to be sick, Joyce, we'd better go back,' she said.

'Don't be silly, Lisa. They're expecting you . . . looking forward to it, I'm sure!'

Lisa wasn't sure. Why would they want her back? She'd done terrible things to them, stolen their belongings, taken money, run off with Jamey and had been an absolute pain in the neck, rude and unhelpful. Why would they want her back?

She took several deep breaths and tried to control her heaving stomach. She tried to think about Mrs Harris and the lost sheep, the one that was found and loved above all the others. She thought about it the rest of the way.

Mr and Mrs Carmichael were at the front door and Jamey was standing on the top step between Mr Carmichael's legs, clinging onto one of them. Lisa couldn't help herself. With a little cry she ran up the drive and crouched in front of him, her arms open. Jamey hesitated, then a big smile spread across his face as he recognised her.

'Eetha! My Eetha!' he squealed, flinging himself at her. At least Jamey forgave her.

Tea-time was rather strained. Joyce left just before Mrs Carmichael served the meal and Lisa felt odd and alone without her. There wasn't much conversation. No-one seemed to know what to say, not wanting to upset anything.

Lisa watched Jamey as he tucked into fish fingers and chips.

'He's a lot bigger,' she said.

Mrs Carmichael smiled. They had been told to be careful what they asked and talked about. Jamey was a safe subject.

'He is, isn't he? He eats like a little horse and he's always up to mischief. He still doesn't say much, to us, but he understands, and he talks to his rabbit ten to the dozen!'

'Did he miss me?' Lisa asked.

'We all missed you,' Mr Carmichael said, then he coughed and had to leave the table to get a handkerchief.

Lisa played with Jamey until he went to bed, helping to bath him then telling him a story as she tucked him in.

'Come down and watch TV with us for a while,' Mrs Carmichael said. 'There's a good comedy on tonight.'

'I think I'd like to go to bed,' Lisa said. 'If you don't mind?' Mrs Carmichael smiled.

'Whatever you want love,' she said.

Lisa could hear them talking downstairs then after a while the talking stopped and there was only bursts of laughter from the TV audience. She didn't feel like laughing. What she really wanted to do was run downstairs and hug them, tell them she was sorry for being such a pain. She wanted them to hug her back and forgive her for all the trouble she had caused.

She wanted to go downstairs, but she didn't. They might push her away and that would be awful, too awful to risk.

Saturday and Sunday passed pleasantly enough. Lisa spent most of her time with Jamey, conscious of two pairs of eyes watching her. She didn't ask if she could take him for a walk; that would be asking too much. She wanted to ask what was going to happen to her but she was afraid of the answer, afraid they would say they didn't want to foster her any more, that she'd have to move, again!

Joyce arrived after tea on Sunday and Jamey cried when Lisa said good-bye.

'They didn't say they wanted me back,' she said to Joyce as they drove away.

'Did you tell them you wanted to go back?' Joyce asked.

'No!'

'Well then, perhaps they were waiting to hear what you wanted.'

'It isn't what I want, though, is it? It's always what somebody else thinks is best, or what they want,' Lisa sighed.

'What *do* you want, Lisa?' Miss Elliot asked the following Wednesday morning. They were waiting outside the Conference room where big decisions were going to be made.

Lisa had spent Monday and Tuesday in a very anxious state, knowing that the outcome of Wednesday's meeting would determine her life, at least for the next few years.

Debbie had given her what she called 'good' advice . . .

'Agree to everything they say, Leez, then as soon as they let you out, leg it!'

'Leg it?'

'Do a runner, stupid! I can't wait . . . soon as I'm out, I'm off!'

'Where do you go?' Lisa asked.

'Anywhere as long as it's a million miles from my dad!'

'Don't you have a mother?'

'Course I have, and I've no time for her either. She married the bloke so it's her own fault if he knocks her about, but he's not thumping me again!'

'He hit you?'

'Hit me? No way, he was just playing! Listen . . . when I was eleven he knocked me downstairs, so I ran off. I've been running ever since! The trouble is they keep catching me and bringing me back . . . to be thumped again! Last time I gave him one back, with something big and heavy! That shut him up for a bit!'

'So what happens now?'

'Residential Care I suppose. Some place with high walls and do-gooders who'll sort out my psychological problems . . . HA! I didn't half give him one. I bet he saw stars! I'd do it again too if he came anywhere near me.'

Debbie was quiet for a minute. Lisa didn't know what to say. Debbie's life sounded so much worse than hers had been.

'Well . . . we'll know on Wednesday,' Debbie went on. 'My case conference day. One thing's for sure, I'm not going home again, whatever they say!'

'Lisa, would you like to come in now?'

There was a polished oval table with several people sitting behind it. Miss Elliot was there, Mrs Thomas, the teacher and three others whom Lisa didn't know. Joyce sat beside her at the front of the table. There was a long silence while they leafed through files and papers then Miss Elliot smiled.

'Well, Lisa, you seem to have settled here with us and your school work has improved quite a lot. Mr Adams is very pleased with your art work, he thinks you have real talent and should continue painting. You seem a lot happier too and the home visit last weekend went well, didn't it?'

Lisa nodded. She didn't know what to say. From what Miss Elliot had said it seemed that they thought she was settled there. Did that mean she would be staying at the centre?

There was a deep ache inside and her stomach churned at the thought. She knew she had to say something because they were all waiting, and the words had to be the right ones.

Behind Miss Elliot was a big painting in an ornate gilt frame. It was a scene with high mountains in the background and a rocky valley in front with a sheepdog herding sheep up a ledge path. At the top was a man in a floppy broad brimmed hat. Underneath the picture on an oval disc was the title 'The Grindelwald.' She couldn't read the painter's name.

It made her think of Mrs Harris and the lost sheep.

'I . . . I'm very sorry,' she said softly.

It was a long meeting. Sometimes it seemed as if she was invisible as they talked about her mother's death and her father's rejection. They nodded and agreed and put forward suggestions as to why she had behaved as she did and how different she had been these last few weeks. Now and again a question was addressed to her.

'What do you have to say about your truancy, Lisa?'

It sounded silly and trivial as she mumbled on about the teachers getting at her and the other girls ganging up on her. It sounded even more stupid when she complained that she hadn't any friends and that nobody liked her . . . and called her names. None of those things was an excuse for the trouble she'd caused everybody.

'It's me, isn't it?' she said, nearly in tears. 'It's me that's stupid!'

Another session of discussion and point making left Lisa to think about school, Miss Dodds and Carrie. Her stomach churned again when she realised that she couldn't think of one occasion when she'd tried to be friends with Carrie or been polite to Miss Dodds. No wonder they hated her!

'What about the fights Lisa, and the bullying?'

Lisa's face was very red as she made excuses like . . . they called me names . . . she gave me a funny look . . . she ignored me . . . she wouldn't give me a sweet, pencil, rubber. It was embarrassing! So was her description of the fight in the dining room and the memory of her rudeness to Miss Dodds.

They didn't mention her taking Jamey and running off. She'd talked to Miss Elliot about it and she supposed they had it all down on paper anyway.

She had to wait outside then, while decisions were made. Joyce was very kind and held her hand.

'I think I'm going to be sick, Joyce,' she said. 'I don't want to go back in. I don't want to know about community care or another foster home!'

At one end of the corridor she waited in were the double doors to the rest of the world. At the other end was the glass box with the watcher inside. Debbie's voice whispered in her head . . . 'leg it Leez, it's the only way!' It was an inviting daydream . . . There was Kev on the pier with a bag full of money, beckoning, and an exciting chase to London with its discos and bright lights, and freedom to do what she wanted . . . but was it?

Miss Elliot came out of the meeting, smiled at Lisa and went into a room opposite. She wasn't there long and Lisa's heart missed a beat when she came out again. Mr and Mrs Carmichael and Jamey were with her. They smiled too as they were ushered into the conference room. Jamey waved.

'What are they doing here?' Lisa whispered to Joyce.

'They are your foster parents . . . they have to be here!' Joyce said, squeezing her hand.

This hadn't happened before. She had been moved from foster homes and placed in others without any discussion.

Lisa sighed. She hadn't gone off her head, kidnapped a little boy and fought two policemen before. This was different.

At last Miss Elliot came for her and she went in to sit in the same chair, this time without Joyce.

Jamey said 'Eetha' and struggled to get down from Mrs Carmichael's knee, hurrying across and scrambling up to put both his arms around Lisa's neck and plant a wet kiss on her cheek.

Lisa wanted to giggle but daren't. She held her breath

and waited for someone to take Jamey away and tell her off.

They didn't.

'Mr and Mrs Carmichael have requested that you be returned into their care, Lisa . . . and by the look of it, Jamey echoes that request.'

There were conditions, but they were drawn up by the board, not the Carmichael's, and there would be a review in one month, just to see how things were going.

Despite her excitement at going home, Lisa sat and listened to the little talk that Miss Elliot gave her, on their own, while the Carmichaels brought the car to the front door and Joyce collected her few belongings.

'Do something for me, Lisa, will you? Each time you feel that temper rising or something doesn't suit . . . count to ten and think! I know you've had an awful time since your mother died but life goes on and we have to make the most of it . . . be the best that we can be.'

Lisa nodded. She wanted to say that it was nobody's business but hers, what she did with her life. That her 'best' was never going to be good enough, but she counted to ten.

It wasn't all plain sailing. That very first tea-time Mr Carmichael droned on and on about pulling up socks and getting down to some hard work to catch up or she'd never have a career worth having and that pop music was the downfall of young people who thought of nothing else but jigging about to jungle drums and hanging about on the promenade messing up the pavements with chewing gum. He talked and talked and Lisa felt like getting up, going out and slamming a door . . . loudly.

But she didn't. She counted to ten and ate her tea.

Mrs Carmichael tried to shut him up but gave it up as a bad job, shrugging her shoulders and grinning at Lisa, who returned her smile and went to help with the washing up.

'We'll never change him, you know,' Mrs Carmichael said as they stood at the sink. 'He likes complaining about "The Youth of Today". You'll have to take it with a pinch of salt. He was just the same with Jennifer . . . nearly drove her up the wall. I remember one time when she came downstairs all dolled up for a youth club disco. She was wearing black leggings and a baggy purple top. "You're not going out like that!" he said, "You look like a plum on a stick . . . and do something with your hair!" Jennifer was hopping mad and stamped upstairs, refusing to go out at all. I don't think she spoke to him for a week!'

'What happened then?' Lisa asked.

'Compromise! The next time she went out she "Did something with her hair" and wore a long coat over the leggings! A lot of life is compromise, Lisa. It's about learning to live together and give and take.'

'I haven't given very much . . . and I took a lot,' Lisa said, bowing her head as her eyes filled with tears.

Mrs Carmichael put down the tea cloth and held Lisa close.

'All in the past Lisa, in the past. Let's start again, shall we?' Lisa nodded.

'I'd like that,' she said. And she meant it. Suddenly Mrs Carmichael wasn't a rather stout woman with stiffly permed hair. She was warm and comfortable to be with, and quite nice looking when she smiled.

The biggest hurdle had yet to be faced. Lisa had to meet with the Governors before she could return to school.

More compromise and more promises! It just happened that the appointment was for eleven o'clock and Mr Carmichael insisted on arriving ten minutes early. That meant they had to cross the Prison Yard at break, when everybody would be going to the dining room for a snack from the tuck shop. It would be just her luck!

It was.

The very first person she saw was Carrie Rogers with her 'hangers on', Joy and Tracy.

Her first reaction was to scowl and make some rude comment but she counted to ten . . . and smiled!

Carrie almost fell over her own feet and collided with Joy as all three stopped in their tracks.

Carrie recovered first and smiled back. 'Hi, Lisa,' she said.

'Hi,' Lisa said, and smiled again. It made her feel good.

The Chairman of Governors was a forbidding figure, a large lady with a flowered hat and rimless spectacles. She read through Mrs Foster's report without saying anything then turned to the Headmistress.

'Do any of the staff wish to add anything?'

One or two of them did and they were asked in, one by one.

Lisa's heart sank when Miss Dodds appeared and sat down without looking at her.

'What's the point?' she said aloud.

'There!' said Miss Dodds, 'That's just what I mean . . . She's rude to me before I've said anything!'

'Because you expect me to be!' Lisa said angrily. 'You make sarcastic remarks when I haven't done anything and you never give me any help when I don't understand. You just say I'm stupid.'

Miss Dodds looked a little uncomfortable. She stood up as she spoke.

'I can't remember how it all started, this antagonism, but I'm prepared to make a new start.'

Lisa counted to ten so that she didn't say 'Big deal!'

Mrs Harris gave Lisa a big smile as she came in and talked a lot about Lisa's sensitivity and interest in her subject. She also said she would welcome Lisa back into her class and was sure that things would be different if people would make allowances when girls were upset. She used the word 'compromise' too.

'We'd all get on so much better if we shared our problems and learned to give and take,' she said. 'We can't all be perfect, can we?' She smiled at Lisa as she said that.

All in all the meeting was a success. Lisa was to return to school the following Monday, with certain assurances . . .

That she would remain on the premises until the end of the school day. That she would attend all the lessons and attempt to make up the missed work. That she would report to Mrs Foster if, at any time, she felt unhappy or unable to cope . . . and that she fully understood that any 'transgression' could result in her being removed on a permanent basis.

'There, that wasn't so bad, was it?' Mrs Carmichael said as they drove home.

'You'll have to pull your socks up now and get down to some hard work, my girl. Nothing comes easy in this life and we all have to . . .'

Mrs Carmichael grinned at Lisa and shook her head. Lisa understood . . . and grinned back.

~ 10 ~

On Saturday morning Lisa was called downstairs.

The call woke her from a very unpleasant dream and for a moment she couldn't think where she was.

She had been trying to cross a very wide river, a river that ran fast between foot-square stepping stones that formed a precarious path to the other side. The opposite bank was so far away that the figures waiting there were tiny, like ants.

At first it was easy, stepping from stone to stone, but further out the water was rougher and the stones were further apart. By the time she was half way across they were so far apart that she had to leap across and it was scary. She looked behind, thinking to go back but the stones had gone. She was alone in the middle of the river and the only way was forward.

Each time she hesitated someone on the next stone called . . . 'Come on, jump. I'll catch you, trust me!' but each time she jumped there were no helping hands and she fell into the rushing water, only just managing to cling onto the stone and haul herself onto it, wet and shivering.

'Come on, Lisa, you must move on, jump! I'll catch

you I promise, trust me!' It sounded like her mother so she jumped but the hands weren't there. They never were there and the opposite bank was always so far away.

She was glad to wake up, even though it was early.

'Will you get dressed and come down when you're ready?' Mrs Carmichael called.

'Eetha, get up Eetha!' Jamey's voice made her smile. He wasn't a thin baby any more, but a chubby talkative little boy. Living with the Carmichaels had done him good, Lisa decided. Perhaps they weren't so bad, really.

'I bet we're all going out!' she told her reflection in the mirror, 'I'd better look my best.'

It promised to be a warm sunny day so she chose her best jeans, a pale blue T-shirt and a white cotton jacket with short sleeves and lots of big pockets.

'Perhaps there'll be pocket money!'

Her hair still looked nice when she brushed it even though the blow-dried wedge had long gone. It was short and shiny and easy to manage.

Lisa felt very happy as she tied the laces of her white trainers and hurried downstairs.

Jamey was watching cartoons on the TV as she passed the lounge door and presented herself for breakfast.

'It's a bit early,' she said, brightly. 'Are we going out?'

There was something wrong.

'Out . . . OUT?' Mr Carmichael said. 'You'll be lucky if I ever let you out again!'

Mrs Carmichael looked worried but didn't say anything. What was so serious?

On the table were two boxes, large cardboard boxes with their tops open.

'We've just had a visit from the police,' Mr Carmichael said. 'They've returned your things – the things you left at the hut. They thought we'd like them back, seeing that most of them are ours!'

Lisa swallowed hard. Why now? Why return them

now after all this time?

'They held them while you were at the centre! The trouble is . . . a lot of this stuff isn't ours!'

He began to pull things out of the biggest box; toys, books, ornaments, jewellery, pens, key-rings . . . all the stolen goods that had made Lisa feel she had something that was hers . . . that was owed to her!'

'Those are my things,' she said between clenched teeth.

'And where did they come from, your things?'

'I bought them.'

'With what, Monopoly money? Come on, Lisa! This is a Crown Derby pill box, these earrings are gold and this is a Parker!'

He held up the sleek black pen and pointed it at her.

'Where did you get the money?'

Lisa was trembling. It was all going wrong, again.

'You said it was all right. You said we could start again . . . this was before . . .'

'This is something else, Lisa. Don't you think you owe us an explanation?'

'I DON'T OWE YOU ANYTHING!'

She knew she did, she owed them a lot, but she'd said it before she'd thought, before she'd counted to ten and there was nothing else to do now but, as Debbie had put it, 'Leg it!'

She turned on her heel and made for the back door.

'Where are you going?' Mrs Carmichael said, her voice rising.

'OUT!' Lisa yelled, and slammed the door.

She was back in the river again!

The pier and the beach and promenade surrounding it were crowded with noisy holiday-makers enjoying the sun. Lisa pushed her way through the crowds and onto the pier, her face red with exertion and anger.

She had run all the way, her feet pounding on the pavement until her ankles ached and she had a stitch in

109

her side but she didn't stop. She had thought about running on into the sea but there were too many people to trip over and to pull her out.

Now, standing by the pier gift shop she took deep breaths to get rid of the stitch and hoped her burning face would cool and fade in the shade of the shop awning.

The window was full of the cheap and gaudy things to attract tourists looking for presents for disliked and remote relatives; ashtrays with the town's crest and cute pottery figures with 'The World's best Grandad' and 'The World's best Teacher' on them.

Lisa strolled inside. People were jostling for position at the counter and the two assistants at the tills were harassed as they tried to cope. The clock behind the counter said ten-thirty. Had she been running that long?'

When Lisa left the shop she had a key-ring with a big brass 'L' dangling on it and a little black and white panda that clung to her lapel with sprung arms. She put it on as soon as she got outside, there was nobody to stop her and the assistants hadn't seen her take them.

She felt better.

'Hey! I haven't seen you around for ages. Where've you been hiding?'

It was Kev, blocking her way and grinning.

'Been away?' he said. 'You one of these rich hotel kids who go off to Tenerife for a couple of months?'

'No,' Lisa said. 'I've been visiting . . . my father in London!' she added in desperation.

Lisa looked at him. His hair was long and hung on his collar in greasy strands. His clothes were scruffy and his face was full of spots. He smelled of cigarettes too and it was awful. How could she have been attracted to him?

He moved closer and nudged her with his shoulder.

'Come to play the machines, have you?' he said with a wink. 'Trust Kev to see you right, eh?'

'Trust you? I don't trust anybody!' Lisa spat out, turning on her heel and colliding with a large figure in a white shirt and light jacket, Mr Carmichael!

'I thought you'd be here,' he said. 'This is where I found you before.'

Kev disappeared into the crowd.

Lisa opened her mouth but remembered, and counted to ten in her head.

'Before you say anything, let's go and have a burger, shall we?' Mr Carmichael said.

There was only one answer to that!

'I've never had a burger for breakfast,' he said. 'But there's a first time for everything!'

'They do bacon and egg muffins. They're nice,' Lisa said quietly. Mr Carmichael collected the order and there was silence as they munched, then, after a gulp of tea he spoke, not angrily, but gently.

'What do we have to do to convince you that we care, Lisa?'

It wasn't what she expected. No lecture or a good telling off. He was smiling at her and she felt like crying.

'Nobody cares,' she said. 'Everybody shouts at me. I'm always in the wrong. I know I'm not very nice . . . rubbish really! Mrs Harris said that if a sheep was lost the shepherd would leave all the others to find it and be happy he'd got it back. I thought "lost" meant "gone wrong" and that if I said I was sorry I'd be forgiven for running away with Jamey and it would all be forgotten. But it doesn't work like that, does it?'

'Let's get one thing straight right now, Lisa. You are not, and never were, rubbish! But, what you're saying is that now you're forgiven you can do what you like for ever?'

Lisa didn't answer.

'Or are you saying that as long as you say sorry afterwards it doesn't matter what you do?'

'No!' Lisa said. 'That wouldn't be right.'

'You can't run away every time somebody criticises you, Lisa. We try to keep you on the right path because we care . . . really. I've made mistakes too and said the wrong things, just like any father would.'

'You're not my . . .'

He held up his hand to stop her but Lisa smiled and went on.

'You're not my father, but I wish you were,' she said.

'Right! Then as your pretend Dad let's go and pay for that panda, shall we?'

Lisa blushed and pulled the key ring out of her pocket.

'No, I'll go and put them back.'

She left him sitting with his carton of tea and crossed the road to the pier and the gift shop. There was no sign of Kevin and the shop had cleared. Lisa took a deep breath and walked in.

One assistant was serving and the other was filling shelves. Lisa spoke to her.

'You were busy and I took these without paying, I've brought them back, I'm sorry.'

'That took a lot of courage, Lisa.' Mr Carmichael said as they drove home.

She was going to need a lot more.

The boxes were emptied on Sunday morning and the Carmichaels' things put back in their places.

'I didn't know we had one of those!' Mrs Carmichael said, picking up an egg whisk to examine it. 'What did you want this for?'

Lisa shrugged. 'Milk shakes?' she said. They all laughed.

The things that didn't belong were put in one box and loaded into the car to be donated to the church for the Summer Fayre.

Lisa went too.

It was the first time she had been inside a church since her mother's funeral.

St Paul's wasn't like the parish church she had gone to with her mother. It was quite new and built of small red bricks that made it look a bit like a supermarket on the outside. Inside it was very light and airy and smelled of polish and at first Lisa didn't like it, but when the organ started playing and the service began she felt comfortable among the new pine pews and the carved Stations of The Cross down both sides of the nave. There was a small semi-circular apse at the end of the nave and a pulpit, also pine, in front of the choir seats.

The windows were filled with brightly coloured glass. There weren't any pictures of saints on them but Lisa thought they were beautiful, one especially. The big window behind the altar was a sunburst of red, orange and yellow with a circle of white light in the centre. When the sun came out from behind a cloud the window was glorious and almost took her breath away.

So did the boy in the pew across the aisle.

After the service Lisa waited at the church door with Mr Carmichael and Jamey while Mrs Carmichael talked to some ladies by the pulpit.

The boy from the pew was standing with his parents by the notice board. He smiled.

Mr Carmichael recognised the boy's parents and moved to talk to them, carrying Jamey.

Lisa followed.

'Hi! I haven't seen you here before,' the boy said.

'I'm staying with Mr and Mrs Carmichael,' Lisa said, feeling very odd inside and sure that her face was red.

'Great!' he said. 'Are you coming to the dance on Friday?'

'What dance is this?' Mr Carmichael asked.

'The Youth Club disco to raise funds for the hospice,' the boy's father said. 'Michael's playing . . . so it won't be for lovers of good music!'

'Do you mind!' the boy called Michael said, 'I think

that's an insult, don't you?'

Lisa grinned, then looked at Mr Carmichael expectantly.

'Would you like to go?' he asked.

Lisa nodded.

'See you there, then,' Michael said as he left with his mother and father.

'I thought nobody liked you,' Mr Carmichael said. 'You could have fooled me!'

Lisa blushed and turned away to meet Mrs Carmichael coming down the path with a bunch of blue irises and coloured freesia.

'My turn to have the flowers,' she said. 'Would you like them for your mother's grave, Lisa? We could go now if you like.'

Lisa cried, muffling the sound with the bedclothes so as not to wake Jamey.

It had been a lovely weekend, the best she'd had for a long time. Mrs Carmichael had helped her tidy her mother's grave and had let her talk about her. She had reassured Lisa that it was not her fault, that she hadn't done anything to cause her mother's death . . . nor could she have prevented it. Mr Carmichael had bought everybody an icecream and had called her 'lovey'. It was as if they were a real family and . . .

Michael Anderson had arranged to see her at a dance.

Perhaps prayers were answered after all . . . if you were prepared to accept the answers, like them or not.

And as for 'lost sheep'! Lisa really felt 'found' and hoped she could live up to the love and care that was being offered.

Mrs Harris had said she should talk to Jesus but she hadn't really tried.

Lisa closed her eyes and re-created the sunburst window that had made her feel good.

'Lord Jesus, help me to understand myself and forgive me for all the bad things I have done. I got a bit lost but I think I'm finding my way again, now that I know I can be forgiven and loved.

Please give me the courage to face Monday morning and help me to be my old . . . no! . . . My NEW self.'

~ 11 ~

Monday morning arrived as Monday mornings will, however much they are unwanted.

It wouldn't have been so bad if it had been raining, but the sky was blue and cloudless, the sort of sky that asked for picnics and long walks on the beach.

'It's exams soon, isn't it? What are you going to do about them?' Mr Carmichael said as he buttered his toast. It was one of the things that irritated Lisa. He always did it the same way, a blob on the corner . . . spread across the top and then down in stripes. Then he always said . . . 'Is this real butter?'

'I never pass anything so there's no . . .'

She stopped at his look, swallowed, and started again.

'I haven't done very well in the past so things can't be any worse,' she said.

'You'll have to try and make up the work, Lisa. Ask one of your friends if you can borrow their work to copy up. Then you can revise,' Mrs Carmichael said.

Lisa nodded. How could she admit she didn't have any friends?

Her uniform had been cleaned and her blouse was really white and nicely ironed. Mrs Carmichael had taken

116

a lot of trouble.

'How do I look?' Lisa said when she was ready. She had looked at herself in her dressing table mirror and, for once, had to admit she didn't look too bad. Her short hair made a lot of difference and she hadn't any greasy spots.

'I haven't one spot!' she said.

'Diet!' Mr Carmichael observed. 'Less of the junk food you young people stuff yourselves with these days. When I was a boy my mother made sure . . .'

'Lisa has to go,' Mrs Carmichael interrupted. 'Are you sure you don't want us to take you?'

Lisa shook her head.

'I'll go on the bus,' she said. 'I'd rather, honestly.'

It was full, as always, and Lisa had to go upstairs. There were juniors squashed three on a seat and a group of older girls right at the back. She could see that somebody back there was smoking and there was a shriek of laughter as she sat down.

She didn't recognise anybody but the juniors sitting near her recognised her. She saw one of them nudge her companion and whisper something then they both turned and looked at her.

'What are you looking at?' said the old Lisa.

They jumped and turned away. Lisa sighed. That wasn't a good beginning!

There were groups of girls all over the Prison Yard and it seemed as if they were all talking about her as she walked past.

'They must be wondering where I've been,' she thought. Then with increasing horror she realised that they must think she had been excluded all this time. They must know she had done something really dreadful!

It was a big temptation . . . to turn and march back down the drive with her nose in the air. It would be easy to be the old Lisa and not care about anybody or anything. But she did care . . . about Jamey and the Carmichaels, and Mrs Harris, and nothing was going to spoil it.

Lisa went in through the front door, under the eyes of half the school. She tried to look straight ahead and not think about the comments and jibes she was sure they were making.

She looked round once, just as she stepped inside and met a pair of eyes in a well known face.

Carrie!

On the spur of the moment and without really thinking about the possibility of rejection, Lisa smiled . . . and Carrie smiled back, waving her hand, just a little, in greeting.

'One stepping stone gained!' Lisa thought.

She stood on the balcony outside the office and watched the school going in to assembly.

Her appointment with Mrs Foster was at nine-fifteen and then she would be marked present and allowed into class. She knew she would have to suffer a lecture!

The Year Head saw the stragglers into the hall and then hurried up the stairs towards her. She always hurried.

'Come in, Lisa,' she said, opening the door to the tutor room. Lisa took a deep breath and went in, standing by the desk and trying to look smart and pleasant.

'Well, Lisa . . . All ready for a new start? Sit down and let's get sorted.'

She was smiling. Lisa didn't think she had ever seen her smiling!

When she left the office she had an exam timetable, a new locker key and a list of the day's lessons.

'In case you've forgotten what you do on Mondays . . . or didn't do!'

Lisa had stiffened, ready to do battle, but Mrs Foster had a big smile on her face and the moment passed.

Not everyone was friendly. Miss Dodds glared at

her on the corridor, walked past her then called her back.

'I don't think you should attempt the exam, Lisa,' she said. 'I can't see you catching up. We've done a lot of work these last few weeks.'

'I'm willing to work every lunch time, if you'll help me Miss Dodds?' Lisa said sweetly, hating every minute of it but determined to change things.

'Are you being funny?' the teacher said, crossly. Then when Lisa didn't stick out her tongue, make a rude sign or tell her to get lost she was covered in confusion.

'Well . . . er . . . I'll do what I can. If you come to my room at one-thirty I'll have some work ready.'

Lisa watched her stomp away up the corridor and when she was sure no-one was looking she did pull a face at Miss Dodds' back.

'You can't change the world in five minutes!' she said to a passing junior who, on recognising the dreaded Lisa Fisher, jumped two feet in the air and came down running.

'What are you doing out of lessons? . . . STAND STILL!' It was the Deputy Head and she was charging down the corridor. The junior froze to the spot as Lisa sighed and counted to ten. It wasn't going to be easy!

The lesson had been going for ten minutes when Lisa arrived at the RE room. She stopped outside and checked that her blouse was tucked in and her hair was tidy. She didn't know what to expect.

Usually, when Lisa Fisher walked late into a room, there was a groan from half the class and comments from the rest. At least the lesson was RE with Mrs Harris.

Lisa opened the door and walked in. For a brief moment she saw again the stepping stones and herself jumping and falling in, then she was facing the class.

They were all grinning and as if on cue and conducted

they said, in unison, 'Welcome back, Lisa.'

It was a heart stopping moment.

'Is this a joke?' Lisa snapped.

She knew it wasn't as soon as she had said it. Some of the girls turned away with the usual disgust and dislike on their faces and some were embarrassed.

'I . . . I'm sorry,' Lisa stammered. 'I've been . . .'

'You've been ill, Lisa, we know,' Mrs Harris interrupted. 'And we are glad to see you back.'

She smiled and nodded to Carrie who came to the front of the room and handed her a card and a little oblong parcel.

Lisa opened it with trembling fingers. Inside was a lovely pen and pencil set and the card was signed by everybody in the class.

'Mrs Harris chose it,' Carrie said.

'A new pen to write on a new page,' Mrs Harris added.

Carrie went back to her desk and picked up a blue file.

'And this is from me,' she said. 'So you'll be able to revise.' Lisa opened the file. There was work there from all the subjects she was taking, all Carrie's notes, photocopied from the time she had been excluded.

Suddenly they were both crying and hugging each other and Mrs Harris was beaming and blowing her nose at the same time.

'Sit-sit-sit!' she ordered, in her usual way. 'Time waits for no man or girl and exams are three weeks away . . . Today . . . Parables!'

Lisa took her place in the desk next to Carrie, took out her new pen and prepared for business.

Mrs Harris read from St. Luke, chapter fifteen.

'*There was a man who had two sons. The younger son said to his father, "Give me now my share of your property so that I can live my own life." So the father divided the property between his two sons. After a few days the younger son sold his share of the land and went away to enjoy his money and do what he wanted. When a severe famine spread over that country he found himself with nothing . . . all his money squandered, and had to ask a farmer for work and shelter. He was set to tending the pigs and saw that they were fed better than he was.*

At last he came to his senses and decided to go back and say to his father "I have sinned against God and you. I am no longer fit to be called your son; treat me as one of your hired workers."

He was still a long way from home when his father saw him; his heart was filled with pity and he ran, threw his arms around his son and kissed him. The father wouldn't hear of making him a servant. Instead he called to his servants, "Hurry, bring the best robe and put it on him. Put a ring on his finger and shoes on his feet then go and kill the best calf so we can celebrate with a feast . . . For this son of mine was dead but now he is alive, was lost but now is found," then the feasting began.'

Mrs Harris stopped there and looked at the class expectantly.

'Well?' she said.

'It's about forgiving,' Joy said.

'It's a bit like the story of the lost sheep,' Lisa said, blushing when everybody looked at her. 'The father is God and forgives the son because he is sorry, like a sheep brought back to the fold.'

Mrs Harris nodded.

'Well done, Lisa.'

'What about the other son?' Natalie Perkins said from the back of the room.

Everybody turned in their desks to look at her. She was leaning back on her chair legs and glaring at Lisa.

Natalie was Form Chairman, a Grade A student and had never ever been in trouble. Lisa had always called her 'Perfect Perkins'.

'He always obeyed his father, worked hard and lived

a good life. Why didn't he get a robe and ring? I don't think that's fair at all!'

'The Bible says that the elder son *was* angry and upset and complained to his father that he had never had a feast made for him in all his years as a dutiful son.' Mrs Harris went on. 'The father answered, "My son, you are always at home and everything I have is yours, but we have to rejoice because he that was dead is alive again, was lost and is found." Does that answer you?'

Natalie still scowled and muttered something to her neighbour and Lisa just heard 'pen set' mentioned.

Mrs Harris just raised her eyebrows and waited. It was one of the ways she got people to talk, to think aloud.

When the silence became unbearable Carrie spoke. 'I think it's about the kingdom of heaven,' she said. 'People who live a Christian life are sure of going there, just like those who do all their work and obey all the rules do well in school, it's expected! When somebody changes for the better it should be celebrated.' She turned to smile at Lisa before she went on. 'I've not been much of a friend, Lisa, but I'll try to change.'

The buzzer went just then and there was a general scramble for the door as Mrs Harris dismissed the class, nodding to Lisa and giving her the 'thumbs up' sign.

It wasn't an easy day. There were comments and questions from all kinds of people, teachers and pupils and Lisa felt herself rising to boiling point several times, but she survived, breathing a sigh of relief at the final buzzer.

'Are you coming on the bus?' Carrie asked as they sorted out homework and checked their lockers were secure.

Lisa shook her head. 'I'll be on the twenty-two in the morning. I'm going to walk home, I want to think.'

'I'm glad we're friends,' Carrie said.

'Me, too. See you tomorrow.'

She couldn't run, not with a schoolbag full of revision,

but she walked briskly so as not to be too late home.

It seemed ages ago that she had asked 'WHY' and hadn't liked the answer.

'*You get what you give, you get what you give*' her feet said as they beat a rhythm on the pavement.

It was true. She had been horrible to everybody. Today all that had changed and people had answered smile with smile and even Miss Dodds had been nice at lunchtime, spending nearly all of it explaining vectors. The class had been nice to her too, after her mistake at the beginning, and it was lovely to be friends with Carrie again. Even the Deputy Head had listened and said, 'Fine, now hurry along to your lesson' when she had explained why she was in the corridor.

It didn't explain why her mother had died or why her father had sent her away but at least she knew now that it wasn't her fault. Some things just happen and although it was very sad it mustn't spoil everything else.

'You have to trust people,' she thought with a shudder as she remembered the awful dream, 'because sometimes they do know what's best!'

Just then she found herself passing St Paul's and remembered the lovely sunburst window, and Michael's dance. That was something to look forward to.

'I'll still need help,' she thought as she walked the last few steps home, 'because I'm stubborn and bad tempered and I don't like being told off . . . but I'm getting better, with a lot of help!'

Lisa walked into the house and closed the door without slamming it. She could hear her family in the kitchen, Mr Carmichael's monotonous drone, Mrs Carmichael's odd comments and Jamey's squeaky prattle.

All talking stopped as she opened the door and went in. Mr Carmichael was sitting at the table, his finger pointed at Jamey who had both hands on his head and his mouth wide open. Mrs Carmichael was by the sink draining the water from a pan of something.

All three heads turned to Lisa and waited.

'Hi Mum! . . . Hi Pop!' she said. 'I'm home!'

Afterword from the author

Over the Edge is based on a true story, for there *are* girls like Lisa in our schools – not always ill-mannered, loud-mouthed and disruptive, but they are there. Many of us have suffered from spoilt lessons, embarrassing confrontations, bullying and punishments caused by someone else's bad behaviour.

Perhaps we moan and complain to each other about an 'out of control' classmate, and turn our backs on the situation.

Perhaps we shouldn't.

Behind every defiant attitude lies a reason, because everything has a first cause, an initial happening that leads into a path of action. Sometimes, because of circumstances beyond control, it is the wrong path, and once on a downward spiral, it is hard to find a way off, without losing face and admitting failure.

Understanding, friendship and steadfast support are not easy things to offer a hard-hitting, angry classmate, who is out to make trouble. But Jesus never said it would be easy!

There is an old saying which advises us not to criticise or draw conclusions until we have walked a mile in the other person's shoes. It means we have to consider how *we* would react to *their* situation.

Lisa's story is told to make you wonder what is behind that angry frown and sharp tongue . . . and when you *do* understand, try to offer a much needed hand of friendship . . . and go *on* trying until it is taken and the spiral is reversed.

Audrey Hopkin.